Guy McLain

CiUniverse®

DRAWING WITHOUT AN ERASER

iUniverse books may be ordered through booksellers or by contacting:

iUniverse
1663 Liberty Drive
Bloomington, IN 47403
www.iuniverse.com
844-349-9409

ISBN: 978-1-6632-0690-9 (sc)
ISBN: 978-1-6632-0691-6 (e)

Library of Congress Control Number: 2020914700

Print information available on the last page.

iUniverse rev. date: 08/26/2020

Chapter 1

Discovering Emma

She was late again. Believe me, this was nothing unusual. One thing you could count on, Mary was always late. Here it was, almost twenty minutes after the hour, and Mary, who was suppose to meet me promptly at 1 p.m., was nowhere to be seen. I stood in the doorway of our favorite meeting place, Serenity Coffee Shop, looking down the street, trying to decide what to do. I could just go in, order a latte and wait, or walk down the street and do some shopping. Downtown Santa Fe is always a nice place to spend a little time during the summer. And today was made to order, perfect New Mexico summer weather, temperature around 85, with a nice light breeze.

As I stood there, unable to decide what to do, and trying to estimate how much time I had before Mary would make her appearance, I spotted an art gallery directly across the street. As a gallery owner myself, I often can't resist the temptation to drop in and see what these little regional galleries have to offer. Who knows why. I guess it just comes down to a love of gloating on how much better my gallery is than all these others. Seeing these small shops is great for my ego.

Another part of my conceit, I suppose, is just the typical New Yorker aloofness coming out in me. I realize that these small galleries in summer tourist towns can't possibly compete with the New York art scene. These tourist shops always have the usual array of conventional landscapes, tacky flower scenes, and a few garish abstract paintings by artists trying too hard to be up-to-date. Many of these places offer as much jewelry as art, since most of the locals are rarely willing to shell out the money for a painting. Many times I go into these galleries just for a good laugh. I know that's terribly snobbish, but I guess it just comes with the territory. After thirty years in the New York art scene I figure I'm a lot less jaded than most.

So I decided to kill some time, walk across the street, and look around this small gallery. As expected, this little shop was overly crowded with paintings, sculptures, and jewelry, especially Native American jewelry, for the tourists. This was exactly what I had expected. There was a large display case close to the front door with a selection of necklaces, bracelets, broaches, and earrings, all designed to appeal to the tourist on vacation.

On a wall deeper in the galley was a group of large light-blue paintings with a few simple brushstrokes in beige scattered about in a haphazard fashion. These paintings were almost abstract, but, due to a vague horizon line through the middle of the canvas, I'm sure many viewers interpreted these paintings as landscapes, maybe a desert scene.

I'm sure these canvases appealed to well-off tourists, but not to rich CEOs and hedge fund managers looking for good investments, the kind of patron I usually work with in my gallery. Buyers here simply aren't able to afford the prices in New York galleries.

I had to admit that over the years I had sold paintings that were almost as bad. Hey, you have to pay the rent. At least the artists I sold in my gallery were a little more consistent and a little more original. This artist, whoever he was, didn't really know what he was doing.

As I took in the wonders of mediocre art that filled this gallery, out of the corner of my eye I glimpsed a painting with a small streak of orange on a dark background. This painting was stuck in the back corner of the gallery, almost hidden from view. I walked back for a closer look and immediately realized that what seemed like a simple touch of orange on a black background was actually a very complex canvas. The background was a strange mixture of black, maroon, and forest green, all subtly applied. The spot of orange, that had caught my eye from a distance, was actually only one of several splashes of orange that gave the painting a spark, or a glow, that radiated off the surface.

As I took in the whole sweep of the painting I began to feel that I was looking into a deep, translucent atmosphere, a dreamlike world of the inner mind. The painting didn't seem to exist on the surface of the canvas but to illuminate a complex interior space. I almost felt that I could walk into this murky world and explore another universe. The effect was absolutely hypnotic.

After several minutes, lost to the reality of the outside world, I was interrupted and brought out of my trance by the young woman who worked in the gallery. "Can I help you?" she said in a high pitched voice.

"Who is this artist?" I blurted out immediately.

"Oh, well yes, interesting painting isn't it." I could tell she was buying time. She had forgotten the name of the artist and was trying to bring it back into her consciousness. Clearly, few visitors asked about this artist.

Finally, it came back to her. "This is the work of Emma Casland," she said proudly.

"Where is she from? Does she live here in Santa Fe?"

"Uh, I'm not sure," the young woman replied hesitantly. "I haven't met her." She paused a moment thinking. "I could call the owner of the gallery. I'm sure he could tell you everything you want to know."

"Do you have any other work by this artist?"

She hesitated again. "I'm not sure exactly what we have. I could look in the back room."

"Please do," I answered immediately.

And then I remembered that I was supposed to meet Mary. She was probably already in the coffee shop.

"Look, I have to meet a friend. I'll be back in a few minutes. Pull out everything you have. And call your boss. I want to know more about this artist."

I was out the door almost before she could respond.

Sure enough, Mary was there waiting. She sat at a corner table sipping her coffee.

"Hi Mary. Sorry I'm late," I said, as I dropped my purse on the table and looked up at the large chalk board showing the list of featured drinks.

After I ordered my cappuccino I put on my gallery owner charm. Mary is one of the artists I represent, and I go out of my way to keep her happy, including flying to New Mexico to visit her at her summer home. Mary is a highly recognized artist who is currently beloved in the New York art scene. The Modern and the Whitney both purchased her work in the last year, and her gallery shows always sell out. Her large paintings are routinely pulling in six figures, and the best part is that she regularly produces a large amount of work to sell to hungry collectors, especially those who are looking for a good investment, and who simply must have one of her paintings for their house in the Hamptons.

Mary is simply a gallery owner's dream and clearly my most lucrative seller. The sales from just one of her shows is enough to keep my gallery in the profit margins for a year. And she checks all the boxes of what a gallery owner wants in one of the artists they represent. Her work is large, colorful, and trendy. Added to all that, she is attractive, dresses fashionably, with just a bit of Bohemian charm expected of serious artists, and, best of all, looks great in photos when the New York Times decides to run a special feature on her.

At gallery openings for her shows she always knows just what to say to the rich collectors who love to mingle with the artist. That is so important when selling art. Artists must strike the right tone. I tell all my artists that when you're talking with a collector you might be bored stiff, but it's your job to play the part of the sophisticated artist. That means being just a little aloof, with just a touch of the Bohemian. But you can't be too scruffy. Collectors don't like a real-life, struggling artist. No, they prefer a cleaned up, slightly ruffled version.

Of course, I remind them repeatedly to never talk about money. I tell them that collectors think that artists don't care about such mundane and worldly things like money. "Artists are supposed to be above that," I tell them. "I know you care about money and would like to be rich, but it's my job to do the bargaining. When you're around collectors, stand around and make obscure references to your artistic process."

After my cappuccino arrived, I found my seat next to Mary. Once we made it through the usual niceties, I asked Mary, "Would you do me a favor? I was just in the gallery across the street and saw this painting. I would like you to take a look at it and give me your opinion."

I took a sip of my coffee. "Have you ever heard of Emma Casland?"

Mary hesitated a moment, "No, I can't say that I have. Is she from around here?"

"I don't know, but I'm about to find out."

After finishing our coffee, and talking about the renovations to her house - she's adding a huge studio so she can make paintings even larger than the gigantic canvases she's already producing - we walked across the street and made our way to the back of the gallery. The young assistant had neatly placed four additional paintings against the wall on the floor underneath the one I looked at earlier.

"Hi again," she chirped happily. "I pulled out the other paintings we have. I think you'll like them."

We walked strait past her, not even acknowledging her greeting, and went directly to the paintings. Mary examined each painting, walking from one to the next. All five paintings I thought were very good, but I waited to hear what Mary thought. I wanted to make sure that these paintings weren't just a product of my delusional dream of discovering the next great American artist.

After several minutes Mary pulled back a couple of steps, but still kept her eyes fixed on the paintings. "I think you've found something," she began. "You're right. These paintings are very good. I wonder who she is. I've never seen her work before, and I know most of the artists around here. I wonder if she's exhibited in New York. I can't believe that an artist this good isn't in a New York gallery."

"I know," I cried out. "That would be my luck wouldn't it. But maybe this is my lucky day. Surely, if she is represented in the city I can't imagine that a top New York gallery would let her exhibit her work in this sorry excuse for a gallery."

I paused and took another glance at the paintings. "One thing's for sure. I'm about to find out."

The young assistant was hovering a short distance away looking hopeful.

I turned to her. "I'll take them all," I said.

"All of them?" she gasped, not believing what she had just heard.

"Yes, all of them," I replied.

Mary laughed. "Wow, you don't waste any time do you. I just wish you were half as enthusiastic about my work."

"Mary, you know I love your work." I was only exaggerating a little bit just to make sure that her ego wasn't bruised.

"You know me Mary. When I like an artist I don't waste any time." I then leaned away from the assistant so she couldn't hear me and whispered in Mary's ear, "These small regional galleries sell work like this for next to nothing. In my gallery these paintings would easily bring in three times as much as they are charging."

I instructed the assistant to wrap the paintings, and within the hour they were packed away in my rental car ready for the trip back to my hotel. After Mary and I parted ways I immediately drove to my hotel. As soon as I was in my room, I picked up the phone and called my assistant back in New York.

"Look up the artist Emma Casland," I instructed. "I want to know everything you can find out about her. Has she sold anything in the city? And is she represented by a New York gallery?"

Within two hours she called me back with the good news. Casland was not represented by a gallery in New York, and there was no record of her selling work in the city. She lived in Santa Fe, not far from the location of my hotel. I was ecstatic. It's certainly not every day that you discover a previously unknown artist with this level of talent. With the good news, I was so excited. I couldn't wait any longer, and so I got on the phone right away and placed the call.

When I got Emma Casland on the phone I explained to her that I was the owner of a gallery in New York, and while here I happened to see her work at her gallery downtown. After telling her how much

I liked the five pieces I had seen there, I asked if it would be possible to see more. She seemed surprised by my call, but happy to hear that someone from a New York gallery was interested in her work. We made an appointment for the following afternoon.

Chapter 2

Visiting Emma

The next afternoon, promptly at 1 p.m., I knocked on Emma Casland's door. When she appeared in the foyer of her apartment I was completely taken aback. I had expected to meet a women in her forties or fifties, or maybe someone even younger. The person who greeted me was much older. I was soon to learn that she was actually 82, although she looked much younger. She was very trim, dressed fashionably in clothes that you would expect to see a woman of 40 wearing, and could have easily passed for someone fifteen, or even twenty years younger.

She welcomed me into her condo, which was in a nice, but a somewhat declining apartment complex. The interior was very bright and modern. We walked through the foyer and down a narrow hallway into a large open room with windows on two sides. This main living area featured stylish furniture in a severely modernist style. Adjacent to the living room was a spacious dining room, where she invited me to have a seat at an old, but tasteful dining room table. On a large serving tray she had placed a block of cheese, an assortment of crackers, cut vegetables, a creamy white dip, and two small cups. She offered me tea or coffee, and invited me to sample the food she had set out.

I have to admit that the last thing on my mind was food at this point. I couldn't keep from staring at the paintings hung all around the apartment. All too often, after I've spotted a painting I like, when I visit the artist's studio, or see a large selection of that artist's paintings, the majority of work simply doesn't live up to the work of art I originally saw. That wasn't the case on this occasion. I was just amazed at what I was seeing around me. Every painting was bold and dramatic, and Casland's brushstroke style was free and intuitive.

Casland was clearly a modernist, since most of her work showed signs of influence from the Abstract Expressionists. I did a quick calculation. Given her age, that would be what one would expect. The fact that the Abstract Expressionists were all the rage when she was in early adulthood must have been important in her formative years. But she was a modernist in a way that wasn't normally associated with modernism. It seemed to me that the best way to imagine her work was to think of her as firmly rooted in a modern tradition that included certain romanticized traits not found in most Modernists.

For instance, she had a decided affinity for Asian mythological stories, most of which I found totally unfamiliar. Elements from these stories could be found fragmented and buried in many of her canvases. In fact, many of her paintings were named after Asian deities, or mythological figures, especially females. But nothing was ever obvious in her work. The viewer had to search the canvas for clues to her visual language. Casland's flair for the subtle and partial disclosure, for a stolen glimpse of some interior dream world, was what turned her paintings into such terrific dramas. There were no shortcuts or overt formulas here. Her best work was organic, improvisatory, and honest.

After a preliminary discussion, we began our walk around her apartment, standing in front of one painting after another, examining the intricacies of each canvas individually. She stood back a little, allowing me to examine each painting as we made our way around the rooms of her apartment. She clearly didn't impose herself, or her artistic ideas. She was perfectly happy to let me absorb her paintings at my own pace, offering just a few hints and ideas as we walked around.

Many artists over the centuries have explored mythological themes, but Casland wanted to approach these themes in a slightly different way. Most of these previous artists were men, and, according to Casland, their renditions of these stories maintained a distinctly male perspective. Casland hoped to bring a woman's sensibility, and a sophisticated feminist perspective, to her work as an artist.

She felt that art history was clogged with way too many themes subtly or overtly reflecting male domination, the age-old stories of men attempting to control women's sexual interests and reproductive rights. Casland felt that these tales were ripe for re-interpretation by female artists today. She also felt that Asian themes were perfect for use by visual artists, since they provided a range of strong images that could be brought up to the current time, and reimagined in a visual language perfect for painting.

The part that Casland seemed to like the best was the ambiguity inherent in these stories. Casland explored the mysteries embedded in the mythological stories she chose in more than two dozen paintings. Some of these works of art were clearly representational, with easily recognized women, and in a few cases men, cloaked in the atmospheric dreamscape of her canvases. Other paintings depicted streaks of gold or red paint running down the canvas.

Many of the women in these particular paintings were nude, and in a variety of positions. Some were standing, others were prone, and still others seemed to be tumbling across the canvas. In a couple of her paintings, she even showed women falling back as if they were in mid-air. Dark shadowy male figures sometimes loomed over these women. But Emma's paintings were never easy to read, and there was never a clear sense of what exactly was happening. She was a master at coaxing the viewer into unraveling the clues and unlocking the narrative of each painting.

I liked that ambivalence very much. To me it was a clear indication that she was pushing her own limits as far as she could. She was trying to explore a visual and emotional realm that was not easily captured.

Anybody can just look at an arrangement of flowers, or a beautiful landscape, and say I want to paint that. There's no risk in that kind of art. But try to explore the murky realm of human sexuality, power struggles between women and men, and the emotions of facing life in it's most turbulent manifestations, and it's clear that the artist can be risking everything.

Other paintings in her Asian mythological series were abstract or semi-abstract. Some canvases in this category would employ a dark patch that could be a figure, but just as easily could be a bush, or simply a shadow. I'm sure that if asked she would say that it was up to the viewer to decide. I particularly liked some of these canvases. The non-representational aspect of these paintings seemed to free her and allow her to fling, splatter, and jab the canvas with a variety of colors. You could tell that she simply loved to work with paint, to use this liquid ooze to create a world that was uniquely her own.

Once she had shown me more than twenty paintings scattered throughout her apartment, she took me down a narrow staircase to her studio in the basement of her condo. I was shocked that an artist creating such original work was forced to work in a cramped basement, and I told her so. She replied that she had no other choice. She simply didn't have the funds to rent a better studio space.

Her story made me realize just how difficult it is for many artists to continue to create and survive. I'm so used to working with celebrity artists with international reputations, selling their paintings for six figures a pop, that I forget that there are thousands of artists working in deplorable conditions, hoping for an occasional sale for a few hundred dollars.

Once we were again seated at her dining room table, she placed another cup of coffee in front of me and sat down. I began my spiel without hesitation.

"I own one of the most successful galleries in New York. I'm in Chelsea, where all the best galleries are located. I represent top artists, many with an international reputation, and some with paintings in museums with good contemporary collections. Several of my artists have paintings in the Modern, the Whitney, and several other major art institutions. I would like you to join our list of artists.

"I can offer you the best representation a New York gallery has to offer. I have a slot for an exhibit of your work available for next Spring, and I would love to feature a selection of your paintings at that time.

"For your first show, I will offer your larger paintings for a range of between $20,000 and $30,000 each, and I know my collectors will think they're getting a bargain. I'll tell them that after the success of this initial show her prices will double, so get them at this price while you can. I'll have them so convinced that I'm offering them a steal that they will literally be begging me to let them buy your paintings.

"If we feature, say 20 of your paintings, and we sell out, which I feel certain we will, you will clear at least $150,000, and you might bring in more than $200,000. Over the next two years, when we mount your second and third shows, I'm sure you will clear more than half a million dollars.

"I have contacts with several top art critics who write for various publications. I feel strongly that I can get them interested in your story, and position you as a major figure who's been totally overlooked until now. All the critics will love the idea of a long undiscovered artist, now in old age, being revived and brought to international attention

"So let me be bold and ask you right now. Would you like to join my gallery? I guarantee, you won't find anyone better at selling your work, or representing your career as an artist."

"I'm overwhelmed," Emma replied hesitantly. "In fact, I feel like I must be dreaming. I thought my chance of getting another New York gallery interested in my work had passed."

"Another New York gallery?" I asked, completely surprised. "I was under the impression that you hadn't exhibited in New York."

"Yes, many years ago, back in the 70s, I had a gallery in New York. It was an exciting time, and being in that gallery was an interesting experience, but nothing came of it. That's why I'm reluctant to sign up again. It didn't go well all those many years ago. But that's a story for another day. I don't want to trouble you with my long tale of woe."

She shook her head and looked at the floor. "I guess I had given up on that possibility years ago. Now, here you are, sitting here at my dining room table. It really seems totally surreal."

"I didn't realize that you had any experience with a New York gallery. My assistant checked and could find no record of your work in New York."

"Well, I'm not surprised," Emma began. "That was quite a number of years ago. And I never had a one-artist show. I was always placed in group shows."

"I must say that I'm really surprised," I replied. "With the quality of your work, I would have thought you would have been a great success. What happened?"

"I don't know," she said as she looked out the window, obviously contemplating the vicissitudes of her career as an artist. "Success or failure in the art world always seems to me to be a combination of at least a little bit of talent and a lot of luck. I guess I just missed out on the luck. Basically, what happened to me was, I guess, fairly common. This gallery owner invited me to show in his gallery, and promised a one-person exhibit, but he went out of business before that happened. After that, I just couldn't seem to find a gallery that would take my work."

"I'm afraid that happens a lot," I said. "The gallery world is a rough business, and a lot of galleries are here today and gone tomorrow. I'm sorry you were a victim of the crazy ups and downs of the art market."

"But this time around is different Emma," I continued. "I'm the owner of a very successful gallery. I've been around for a number of years, and I have no intention of going out of business anytime soon. Last year my gallery sold more than ten million dollars worth of art. Two of the artists I represent sold more than a million dollars in art each."

"This just all seems like a very bizarre dream," Emma stated, continuing to stare out the window.

"It isn't a dream Emma," I replied. "This is very real. Your work is extremely good, and deserves to be seen, to be understood, and I can do that. I can make your art, all the work you've done over so many years, known to the art world."

Now she was looking down at the table, watching her own hands slowly turn and twist the coffee cup she held. I could detect a nervous twitch in her fingers as she thought over what I was proposing. Everything was so sudden, and in my usual style, I had thrown a lot at her all at once. But I was sure she wanted what I had to offer. What artist wouldn't want this. Yet, she must have realized that this could change her life drastically, and that thought, especially after she had given up on that dream, must have scared her. Here she was in her eighties, not a time we expect to have a chance at fame and fortune. It had to be disconcerting.

"If I were smart I would probably ask you to go away and say thanks, but no thanks. I worry about getting my hopes up yet again just to see them dashed when my paintings fail to sell. But I guess I'm just crazy enough to try it again." She took a deep breath. "I guess, against my better judgement, that the answer is yes," she said. "If you want to show my paintings in your gallery I guess I'll let you have anything you want."

"Wonderful!" I said, almost jumping out of my chair. "You won't regret this. You are about to become a famous artist, and so many people are going to have the experience I just had, the opportunity to see your wonderful work. I'm so excited."

"So what do I do now?" she asked. Do I need to ship the paintings up to New York? I'm afraid I'm totally unfamiliar with how this whole process works these days. My guess is that things have changed a lot since I was last in a New York gallery."

"Don't worry about a thing," I exclaimed. "We will take care of everything. I will have my assistant send you a contract immediately. When you get it all you need to do is look it over, make sure it meets all the requirements that you want, and if it does, just sign it, and send it back to us. When we're ready for your paintings, and I'm certain that we will want to get them to the gallery very soon, I will send a crew down here to carefully pack everything. I have an excellent crew of art handlers. They will make sure that all your paintings make the trip in excellent condition."

I reached out and touched her arm. "But we're getting ahead of ourselves. I would love to have you come to New York and see the gallery. I want to introduce you to my staff, and I want you to be able to see where your art will be shown. I also want to be able to talk with you more, just like we're doing right now. If I know more about your background I will be able to develop a marketing plan and a strategy to present you in a way that will position your art in the best possible light for the critics and for our collectors."

I continued, getting more excited by the minute. "Collectors are funny in a way. They are basically very insecure, especially when it comes to buying art. Even though they would never admit it they wouldn't know a good painting if it slapped them in the face. They rely on me to tell them what to buy."

I smiled and gave her a wink. She returned the smile, knowing that I was sharing an inside joke between gallery owner and artist. "Of course, I can't just come out and say 'buy this painting.' I have to make them think that they have superb taste, and that they are the ones discovering these rare jewels, these wonderful paintings. I casually mention a few ideas, maybe throw in a fact or two about the artist's background, and soon they're giving me a lecture about how good the art is. And I'm more than happy for them to think that they came up with all these brilliant insights about the artist."

I then leaned back and took on a smug demeanor. "Of course, I stand there and act amazed that they could be so perceptive. I complement them on their brilliant insights, and then take their check with, quite often, a nice six figure sum on it. It's all in a day's work."

Emma laughed. "From what I've seen today I'm sure you're re quite good at this. But I must ask you. Do you help them find a painting that matches their couch?" She giggled and looked at me with a sly wink.

"On no, I would never do that," I exaggerated sarcastically with a big wave of my hand. "Remember, I deal with just the most sophisticated and discriminating buyer," I said facetiously.

She laughed with a delightful giggle that reminded me more of a young girl than that of an elderly lady. I could tell she had a wonderful sense of humor, which made me like her all the more. I felt immediately that I was going to enjoy working with her.

Now that we had had some fun laughing about the Philistines, I felt we were truly becoming good friends. And I realized that I really liked Emma Casland. She was certainly a serious artist, and a talented one, but she was also a nice person, able to laugh and let her guard down with a good joke. I have to say that this isn't always the case.

It might be surprising to many, but artists can be real jerks. I've certainly known my share of artists who could be malicious and cruel. In fact, it never ceases to amaze me that artists who have so much talent, who can create such memorable works of art, can be so malignant in life. But Emma wasn't that way at all. I could tell that she was generous and magnanimous.

Although I was enjoying my visit immensely I had spent almost three hours with Emma. I felt that this had been an excellent first visit, but it now seemed that it was time for me to go.

"Well, this has been a wonderful visit," I began. "But I really should be going. I've taken way too much of your time."

I stood up and took one more look around the room adorned with her paintings. "Let me suggest, as I said earlier, that we meet in New York in a few weeks. I'm only staying in Santa Fe for the rest of the week, and will then be back in the City. I have a show opening in early September, and I simply must devote time to preparing for it, but as soon as that show opens I'll have time for us to meet."

"I guess I can get a flight to the city then," Emma said.

"Oh no, don't even think about it," I interrupted. "We will send a first-class ticket for you. I know an excellent hotel just a few blocks from my gallery where you can stay. We will make the reservations for you and we will cover the cost. When you come I'll show you the gallery and introduce you to my staff, and we can talk more about planning your exhibit."

"This is all simply bizarre," Emma replied. "I'm still processing it all. After all these years..." She hesitated, trying to find the words. "After so many years of rejection, of barely being able to get a couple of small galleries to even consider showing my work, it seems amazing that a New York gallery wants my paintings again after all these years."

"Well," I began, "after what I've seen today it doesn't seem incredible to me. Rest assured, the days of not being able to show your work are over. I"m going to see to everything. All you have to do is simply continue creating wonderful paintings." On that note, I said my goodbyes, got into the car, and drove back to my hotel.

Chapter 3

From Spoiled Rich Girl to Cutthroat Gallery Owner

In mid September we made all the arrangements for Emma Casland's visit. We scheduled her flight and reserved a room in a nice hotel not far from the gallery. She flew into the city on a mid-week afternoon, and we had a car waiting for her at the airport.

Once she arrived at the gallery, I showed her around, walked her through the exhibit we had on display at that time, and introduced her to my staff. She didn't seem to like the exhibit, and I couldn't blame her. I wasn't that crazy about it myself. The painter we were featuring was a young artist who was the sensation of the moment, and it was my job to act like he was the next Picasso. But with Emma I dialed back the usual sales pitch dialogue I used on collectors. I knew that if I exaggerated she would pick up on it right away.

Even though she wasn't keen on the current exhibit, she seemed to like the gallery and the staff. I had told all my employees to roll out the red carpet for Emma, and they followed through accordingly. They treated her like royalty for the whole time she was in the gallery, and I could tell that it made her somewhat uncomfortable. She clearly wasn't used to this kind of attention and flattery. To me, seeing an artist being told how wonderful they are every five minutes, and it not go to their head, was like a breath of fresh air. It's rare to see an artist who is actually humble. Most of my artists walk in here like they're god's gift to the universe, but not Emma. At times, she seemed visibly disturbed by all the attention.

After the tour of the gallery we went to a nice French restaurant a few blocks down the street. There we enjoyed a good meal and an expensive bottle of wine. As soon as we had ordered she asked me about my background. "So tell me how you got into the art business," she asked. I could tell that over the weeks since our first meeting she had developed a strong curiosity about me.

I told her that I was a fairly typical New York rich kid. She laughed at that. I explained that my father worked on Wall Street and made way too much money. My mother was basically your garden variety Upper East Side socialite. She was on all the right boards and made sure to volunteer at all the right charities.

"I grew up bored and rebellious and entitled. I thought the whole world was made for me. I guess, in many ways, I was a typical teenager, but being rich in New York didn't help. My mother tried to control me by being too strict, my father tried to keep me in line by being too indulgent. Both strategies proved largely unsuccessful."

I told Emma how I went to a series of private schools and succeeded in getting thrown out of one of them when I was fifteen. I did drugs, stayed out all night at parties, and generally did the absolute minimum to get passing grades. I told her that my parents were driven almost to despair by the time I was a senior in high school. "But somehow, I'm not sure how, I made it to high school graduation without killing myself on drugs, or getting pregnant."

Emma laughed. "Wow, knowing you now, I never would have thought you could be such a hell-raiser as a kid."

"I'm sorry to say that I was a real brat then. Of course, even though I'd been a terrible student and a constant troublemaker, my parent's money and influence succeeded in getting me into Mount Holyoke

College in Massachusetts. I think my father had to cash in a whole lot of favors to get me in, and I wonder now if he thought I was worth it. But, of course, that's what parents do. My parent's money worked wonders."

I went on to explain that for the first year there I was totally lost, but I knew I had to stay in school. As I've said, my father was indulgent, but there were limits to his patience. He told me the day he drove me to college that if I wanted to keep my allowance coming I had to stay in college and stay out of trouble.

Then I told Emma how I discovered art. "In my second year, not knowing what else to take, and choosing most of my classes almost by chance, I signed up for an art history course. Within just a few weeks I was hooked. I loved looking at the paintings projected on the screen in the front of the class, and I loved the discussions about the works of art. Understanding the process by which an artist took an idea, and translated it into a painting or a sculpture, simply fascinated me."

I went on to explain what really appealed to me about art history. "Artists, or at least what artists created, were clearly valued by people like my parents and their dinner party friends. Yet, artists were also outsiders. At that time, being very young and naive, I believed the stereotype that artists didn't seem to care so much about money and status. I thought they were all subversives, yet they had something the rich valued and desired."

Of course, I now realize how completely misguided that perspective was. Artists can be just as greedy for money and fame as any Wall Street broker. But I didn't know that at the time. In the unassailable logic of a nineteen year old, I thought I had found the best of both worlds. I could go against my parents and their world, and yet still be accepted, and even encouraged by them.

I then told Emma about a dinner party I attended during my sophomore year, when I was home during school break. One of my parent's friends, trying to find something to discuss with a clearly bored teenager, asked me what my major was. When I announced that I had chosen art history there were murmurs of approval around the table. "I can still remember the evening as if it was yesterday, my mother beaming a great big smile and a look of love like I hadn't seen since I was a toddler."

Emma laughed. "You're story is fascinating. I hope you don't mind me laughing, but I can just picture the scene you describe."

I went on to tell her of life after college. I told her of how I lived the life of a typically entitled woman in her early twenties who really didn't know what to do with herself. I traveled around Europe for awhile, but I really didn't know how to take advantage of the experience at that point in my young life. The only thing that really paid off from my time in Europe was the fact that I visited a lot of museums while I was there. "Eventually, I got tired of traveling," I told her. "I came back to New York and quickly fell into a social life of way too many parties, way too much drinking, way too many drugs, and way too much casual sex with way too many men."

Then I explained how I got into the art business. "With an art history degree, and a couple of phone calls from my father, I was successful at getting a job as a receptionist in an art gallery. The job was the lowest position in the gallery, and the pay was meager. My main responsibility was smiling at visitors when they walked in, and running to get coffee for the other staff. As you can imagine, the art world was extremely sexist in those days."

Actually, it's extremely sexist now. We're just much better at covering it up. I can't tell you how many times one of the men on staff, or rich collectors visiting the gallery, felt free to pat my bottom, or touch my breasts. There were even collectors, some with their wives standing close by, who would ask to meet me after work. Some were amazingly persistent even after I said no emphatically several times.

"But I loved being part of the art world, even if I was on the periphery," I explained. At that time all the cutting edge galleries were in Soho, and I wanted to be in the middle of the action. So I moved out of my parents Upper East Side apartment, and found a small place just a few blocks from where I worked.

I then explained how I was soon hanging out with all the misfit artists and their friends. This was both good and bad. It was good for making important contacts, and I was also learning more about art than

I ever learned at college. It's amazing what you absorb just by having a beer with an artist, or hanging around an artist's studio. I began to develop a much better understanding of the creative process, and I think I developed a much better eye for a good painting during this period. Some of my artists friends really helped me cut through the crap and begin to perceive what really made a work of art successful.

The bad thing about hanging out with artists, at least for me, was the very characteristic that attracted me to them in the first place. Artists, especially younger artists, can be a little wild, and tend to eschew living regular lives, which was exactly how I wanted to go about living my life. Since every artist, and everyone around the artists, felt that it was absolutely imperative that they prove how nonconformist they were, we were all trying to look and act as anti-establishment as possible. We all wanted to prove that we were anything but a typical middle class American, which, of course, most of us were.

The problem for many of us was that being unconventional, or artistically experimental, is a lot harder than it looks. "Think about it," I told Emma, "if you haven't come up with a stupendously new style of painting, that makes all the other artists in New York seem so old-fashioned, or if you're simply a flunky art gallery receptionist, like I was, how do you prove your nonconformist credentials? How do you keep from looking like a typical rich kid who's daddy got her a job in an art gallery?"

As anyone might anticipate, most of us weren't really that hip and sophisticated, but we were desperate to look like we were. So we all resorted to dressing as weirdly as we could, acting totally crazy at parties, doing drugs to help us come up with ways of looking even crazier, and sleeping around with other people to show how liberated we were.

I then told Emma about my first marriage. "Eventually, from sheer exhaustion, if nothing else, I got involved in a long-term relationship with a young artist, and after a rather tumultuous courtship, we got married. My mother wasn't happy, as you can well imagine. She thought he was a complete idiot and not all that talented when it came to painting, which I now have to admit was largely an accurate assessment.

But I think she accepted my decision to marry simply because she believed that marriage might settle me down and stabilize my life."

Of course, that was wishful thinking. I soon made the mistake of getting pregnant. After the baby arrived we tried to become a nice stable couple with a young child, but my creative genius husband just couldn't handle it. He was trying so hard to make it in the art world. All the domestic drudgery of taking care of a baby went against his idea of himself as a visionary artist. He felt that changing diapers was simply beneath his dignity. Women, on the other hand, according to his enlightened perspective, were suppose to do that sort of thing.

"Yea, I really liked changing smelly diapers. It was what I always dreamed of doing."

At this point Emma was holding her hand over her mouth to keep from breaking out in laughter. "I can identify with that. I had two children, and let me assure you, my husband didn't change diapers either."

I then told her that by the time the baby was walking he was gone, blaming me for everything that went wrong right up to the minute he walked out the door. "However," I said, "all in all, having a baby turned out to be good for me. It certainly made me focus my life in ways it had never been before. And I truly loved my beautiful daughter."

But she also turned out to be a real life lesson. My mother commented when the baby was still a toddler, "You're about to understand what I went through trying to raise you."

Of course, she was right. My daughter turned out to be just as feisty as I had been, and just as difficult to handle. The teenage years were especially grueling for both of us. The difficulties she faced, coming to terms with her sexuality, made the usual teenage transitions even more traumatic. She now lives in California with her female partner. I usually see her once or twice a year when I have business on the West Coast.

I then told Emma how I became a gallery owner. "After a number of years devoted primarily to raising my daughter, and working in various odd jobs more or less related to, or on the periphery of the New York art scene, I met Leon Agostini, at a gallery opening."

He ran one of the biggest and most successful galleries in the city at that time. I attended many openings in those years when my daughter was young. Keeping contact with the art world was the one thing that kept me sane. Yet, I had never met the famous Leon Agostini. Then, as I stood with a group of my artist friends, there he was, right next to me. One of my group introduced us, and before I knew it he was asking me to join him for a drink after the opening. As these things go, one thing led to another, and six months later we were married.

I really wasn't that excited about the prospect of getting married again. I held the idea that once was enough, and that I had learned my lesson. But Leon was the kind of person who didn't take no for an answer when he wanted something, and he had decided that he wanted me.

I was in my mid-forties, he was in his mid-sixties, and although we were separated by many years, it was a good marriage. There wasn't much passion, but I wasn't really looking for that anyway. I told Emma that, "I had experienced plenty of passion in earlier relationships, and I have to say, for the most part, it's way overrated. Sure, it feels good when you're in the middle of a steamy relationship. But passion can be a volatile substance that can blow up in your face. Sometimes, just feeling happy with someone can be much better. I feel that's what I had with Leon. What we had together was comfort. It was a comfortable arrangement."

Emma leaned over the table at this point, and with a deeply empathetic look in her eye, told me she understood completely. "Yes, I know exactly what you're saying. I too began looking for passion when I was young. At a certain point, after all the misery that love brings, just being with someone who understands you, and cares about you, and supports you, is so much more important."

I went on to explain how much I learned from him. He was really great at running a gallery. Leon was equally good with collectors. He could make a collector think they were getting the next Mona Lisa. He also had a great eye for new talent and new trends. He could smell a new style emerging in the art world quicker than almost any other person in the business. That gave him a tremendous advantage over the competition.

Once a new trend was on his radar screen, he visited dozens of artist's studios, looking for the painters or sculptors who were working in that new vein. Then, he would quickly sign up four or five artists who seemed to be the most representative practitioners of that new style. A short time later Leon would open a big show with all these new artists. His gallery would be the hottest spot in the art world for the next six months.

Even though I was his wife, and didn't have an official position with the firm, I made a point of being at the gallery as much as possible, and I tried to attend every single one of his openings. I felt I was learning so much just seeing how he ran things from day-to-day. And I really loved hanging around his gallery. It was such an exciting place to be in those crazy times.

Regrettably, we only had a half-dozen years together. He died of a stroke at 71. I explained to Emma what I felt happened. "He seemed to be in such good health, but maybe he worked himself to death. He often put in twelve hour days, and rarely took time off. In the end it was abrupt. One day he was working in the gallery, and the next day he was dead."

Of course, I inherited the gallery and his stable of artists. Almost everyone thought that it was only a matter of time before the business collapsed, and I have to admit that I lost several artists that first year. But I was determined to keep the gallery alive. In fact, I was committed to making it grow.

As it turned out my lessons under the master paid off. I was actually as effective in many ways as Leon had been. I had finally found something that I was good at and truly loved to do. Before long I was recruiting new artists, many of whom were the hottest new talents in the city. And I worked hard to represent all my artists properly, making sure their work sold at premium prices. It often wasn't easy.

"Let's face it," I told Emma, "the New York gallery scene is as vicious an environment as any type of profession out there. I used to think that my father's line of work on Wall Street was cutthroat. I would be willing to wager that the gallery business would make Wall Street look like a walk in the park in comparison. But I was determined to beat the competition at every level, and, as I seem to have proven over the years, I have a knack for cutting throats with the best of them."

My contacts with the Wall Street world of my father helped as well. More than once I borrowed his Rolodex and used it to drum up business. It didn't take me long to realize that all those boring dinner parties I was forced to attend as a child were now paying off. I knew how the rich thought, and I knew how to sell to them. Within a very short time all those naysayers, who had predicted my demise, were eating their words.

"After all these years I feel good about my record of running the gallery," I exclaimed. "I've helped a lot of artists find both wealth and fame. After many years of self-destructive behavior, of living a totally rudderless existence, giving a helping hand to deserving artists is, quite possibly, the one positive thing I've contributed to this crazy world."

At this point I reached for my wine glass and said, "That's enough about me. In fact, that's way more than enough."

"No, no," Emma exclaimed emphatically. "That was fascinating. You have such an interesting story. Despite all the problems, it must have been exhilarating to be in the center of the art world."

"I guess so," I replied. "I don't know how good it was in the early years, when I was still trying to find myself, but after I had established my gallery and was off to a good start, I loved every minute of it."

I finished the last of the wine, set my glass on the table and then pushed it aside. "Now that I've told you my story in exhausting detail, I want to hear your story. And don't leave anything out."

"Well," she waved her hand at the air between us, "my life hasn't been half as glamorous."

"I'm sure your wrong," I contradicted. "My guess is that there are a lot of events in your life that made you the artist you are. I feel that we've already become good friends, and as a good friend I want to really get to know you. You seem fascinating to me. Maybe it's simply my interest in the life of an artist. I've always been extremely curious as to how artists think and work and feel, and how they live their lives."

Emma paused and looked down at her hands, thinking about how she wanted to reply to my request. "I understand your curiosity," she began, "and I'm more than willing to tell you about my life. But, to be honest, I feel that in order to help you understand my journey, what turned me into an artist, I need to tell you a very long and complicated tale."

She now looked strait at me in order to judge my real interest. "I'm afraid, there are more than a few events in my life that are..." at this point Emma hesitated and looked out a window, deep in thought, "Well, I guess there are many things that took place over the years that are unsavory, even sordid. I'm not sure you want to hear all that."

"I understand what you're saying," I replied. "I don't want you to feel that you need to reveal to me anything you're uncomfortable talking about. Frankly, I'm not surprised. I would even go so far as to say that I expected that to be the case. I have yet to know an artist who hasn't suffered through trauma at some point in their lives. I'm afraid it goes with the territory. Maybe every life has it's sordid moments, to use your words, but artists seem to get an extra large dose of life in all it's complexities. Regrettably, or ironically, that seems to be the thing that makes them artists. So I invite you to tell me what you feel comfortable revealing. I want to understand what made you an artist."

Emma looked off in the distance once again, as if she were remembering her whole life in one powerfully concentrated moment. "Well, if you insist here goes."

Chapter 4

Emma Casland's Story: The Early Years

I was born on a small dirt farm in the middle of Texas back in 1930. The farm was very isolated. The closest real town, a little place called Hamlin, with a population of no more than 2,000 people, was about ten miles away. My grandfather owned the farm, but during the years of the Great Depression few farms could support a family, and my grandfather's was no exception. Every season created a struggle for the family to bring in enough revenue to keep the place operating, and my grandfather constantly faced the possibility of bankruptcy.

My grandfather was used to that hardscrabble life. He was one of those crusty Westerners who had withstood so much through the years. He endured a number of setbacks over the decades, but just kept on going. He was born in Kansas in 1870, the son of a Methodist minister who moved to that state prior to the Civil War. Long before my grandfather was born, his father, an idealistic and deeply religious man, inspired by Abolitionist leaders he had heard speak in New England, moved his entire family from Massachusetts to the barren prairie in the

1850s in order to fight those who wanted to make Kansas a slave state. Family lore claims that my great-grandfather participated in some of the battles that took place between pro-slavery and anti-slavery groups in the years leading up to the Civil War.

Just a few years later, during the time that the Civil War raged across the nation, the Land Grant Act of 1862 was passed by Congress. According to the provisions of this act, anyone who was willing to settle and farm a section of land on the vast prairies of the American West for five years would be granted ownership of a 160 acre plot. My great-grandfather, seeing an opportunity, staked his claim on a nice section of land outside Lawrence, Kansas and became a successful farmer, in addition to his activity as a minister.

My grandfather was born on that farm during the bleak winter months of 1870. As he grew into a muscular young man, he learned every aspect of farming the difficult prairie dirt. But the farm wasn't large enough to support so many children, and my grandfather, being the youngest of six boys, was forced to start out life working a variety of odd jobs on other men's farms. He left his father's home at fourteen years of age, and began migrating from job to job for many years.

When the government decided to open up portions of the Oklahoma territory, just south of Kansas, for settlement by people hungry for a piece of land, my grandfather saw his chance to own a farm like his father's. When the day finally arrived he, like thousands of others, took his place along a vast line set up by the government. When the shot rang out, he joined the stampede into the new territory.

He put down stakes on a dry stretch of land in the middle of the Oklahoma plains, built a dugout in the side of a hill for shelter, and began his life as a farmer struggling from year to year. After a couple of difficult seasons my grandfather met and married a girl, my grandmother, who lived on a neighboring farm.

I remember my grandmother joking that the only reason she married my grandfather was because he was the only available man within ten miles of her parent's farm. She often hinted that she was very naive, and had no idea what married life would be like. I got the distinct feeling that their marriage was difficult at first, and that they had suffered through a hard period adjusting to one another. Eventually things settled into place. My father was born a couple of years later in a one-room sod brick house that my grandfather built.

Farming in Oklahoma in the first decades of the twentieth century was always risky, and all it took was one bad season to send a farmer into bankruptcy. In 1922, after almost thirty years of working this unforgiving land, my grandfather's crops failed, and at the age of 53 he lost the farm the following year. As he had in his youth, he was again forced to drift from one job to another. This continued for several years until he finally succeeded in acquiring another farm near Hamlin, Texas, just one year before the stock market crash of 1929.

Since the farm barely provided a subsistence income, his sons, including my father, had all taken other jobs to supplement the family's earnings. My father was lucky. When so many men were out of work, he had somehow held onto a job as a truck driver making deliveries to small grocery stores in the region.

It didn't pay much, but he and my mother were making enough to survive by living on the farm with my grandparents. My mother didn't like living in her husband's family home, but she really had no choice. Occasionally, I heard her complaining about it, and on a couple of occasions, she even threatened to return to her parent's home. My father's bouts of drunkenness didn't help matters. In fact, their marriage seemed troubled from the very beginning, and from as early as I can remember, their fights were a constant element in their relationship.

My father's brother (my uncle) and his wife were also living with us, which made the house very crowded. I still remember the rickety old farmhouse as a swarm of activity. It seemed like there was always someone coming in or going out. But I had never known anything else, so I took it as simply the way things were.

And I was very happy growing up on this isolated farm. The adults always seemed worn and tired, with long faces wrinkled with worry and stress. But the children, insulated from the brutalities of the Great Depression, went about the business of growing up, playing in the fields, and making up imaginary stories inspired by the small collection of books read to us in the evenings. A host of fairy tale characters enlivened our impoverished existence.

It's funny when I think back on that time now. Although we were very poor, I never felt poor in those early years of my youth, and I don't think the other kids did either. The rest of the world didn't exist beyond the small orbit of our existence. I didn't know what life was like beyond the little town of Hamlin we occasionally visited to pick up groceries and supplies. It was a very small world, but I thrived in it.

Since I was the oldest of the children, it was my job to make sure the younger kids made it to the little one room schoolhouse down the road. I loved school. I looked forward to it every day, and learning came easily to me. Before long the teacher was recruiting me to help the kids who were struggling with their lessons. I practically taught my younger brother to read by myself.

This was also the time that I first learned to draw. Our teacher would often let us draw if we finished our school work. Since our assignments always seemed easy to me, and I was able to finish them quickly, I often spent a good portion of the school day creating all sorts of pictures.

I absolutely loved to draw. At first I just enjoyed covering the paper with all the different colors in the crayon box, but after awhile I grew a little more committed to depicting scenes realistically. Soon my teacher began to notice my pictures, and complemented me on many of them. I was so happy when she chose one of my drawings and hung it up on the wall behind her desk.

Of course, I was very committed to the idea of drawing "realistically" at this time. Yet, somehow I sensed that my creations were more interesting - at least to myself - if I employed a little creative license as it were. Rather than simply color the leaves of a tree green, I would add in some red, and maybe some blue or purple. I can still remember other kids telling me that leaves are green, not purple. They would ask me why I was adding those other colors to a perfectly good drawing of a tree. I didn't know how to answer, but for some reason I liked those supposedly "weird" drawings better.

Of course, at that time, I never thought of these early forays into art-making as serious, or preparations for a career. I would have been astonished to hear that there were people in the world who actually made money selling their art. None of the adults around me introduced such a preposterous idea. They would have been as equally surprised by the idea of art as a career option as I would have been. No, in those days my drawings were strictly a recreational activity, something fun to do when other work was finished, and I gave it no more thought than that. But now, when I look back at that period in my life, I can't help but feel that this was an indication that I was destined to become an artist.

My insulated existence in rural Texas came to an abrupt end when I was ten years old. I sometimes think back to that time and wonder what it would have been like if my life on a small Texas farm had continued uninterrupted. I was very happy living the way I was, and I could have easily spent the rest of my childhood attending that small school and living in my grandparent's house. But, somehow, I don't think I would have become an artist if I had stayed on the farm.

Ironically, happiness in childhood rarely provides the right soil to nurture an artist. It's counter intuitive, and maybe a little sad I guess, but it seems to me that almost all artists have to experience at least a little unhappiness in childhood in order to become a significant artist as an adult. Comfortable childhoods rarely lead to meaningful and sophisticated creative expression in adulthood.

It was the fall of 1939, just before World War II, when my comfortable and idyllic childhood came to an abrupt conclusion. I remember that it was a beautiful autumn day, sunny, with a crisp, cool chill in the air. I was sitting in the living room helping my brother with his math homework. I saw my father walking up to the front door, slowly and methodically. I took one look at his face and knew that something was wrong.

I sat perfectly still, not knowing what to do or how to react. All of a sudden I became acutely aware of everything around me. Every object in the room became more vivid, and every sound, no matter how quiet, seemed amplified. I can remember my brother looking up at me with a questioning expression, not understanding why I had suddenly stopped explaining the math problem he had been trying to solve.

My father opened the front door, walking straight through the living room and into the kitchen without looking at the two of us sitting there on the floor. I could hear my mother greet him, but then change her tone immediately. "What's wrong?" I heard her say in a hushed tone.

There was silence, a silence that seemed way too long. "I lost my job," I heard my father say in a soft, even tone, without emotion. "The company is cutting back. I don't have a job," he continued.

Silence again. After a few seconds I heard my mother move and adjust her stance slightly. "What are we going to do?" she whispered. "Your brother isn't working either. Now, with both of you out of work, how is your father going to be able to keep the farm?" she questioned.

"I don't know," my father replied, with a flat tone that seemed resigned to an oncoming tragedy.

All of a sudden I knew that my world was about to change drastically, but I had no idea what substance or shape that new existence would encompass. The whole house seemed to loose its solidity and move in liquid motion around me. Although I was sitting on the floor, I stiffened my arm against the hard wood surface for stability.

The next few weeks seemed filled with agitation. All the adults in the house kept trying to tell me that everything was fine, that I didn't need to be concerned, and that everything would work out for the best in the long run. I didn't believe them. I knew that they were just telling me these little white lies so I wouldn't worry. I could see in their anxious faces and whispered conversations that this was a crisis, and that they were just as confused about the future as I was. I don't know why adults are always so intent on hiding things from children. It almost never seems to work. Kids see right through the lies, and probably feel even more anxious knowing they aren't being told the truth.

Soon my parents were having arguments almost every day. Sometimes they simmered on for hours, with a low intensity that seemed to heat the very air around them. Other times they escalated into open warfare. On one occasion the fight grew so intense that my mother slapped my father after an especially rancorous exchange. After the blow landed with a sharp wack there was a pause of total stillness between the two as they stared at each other.

Then the anger in my father boiled to the surface. I could see his hand turn into a hard, red fist and fly up at my mother. The punch landed squarely on the side of my mother's face, and was delivered with such force that she flew across the room, furniture and lamps and everything on the furniture, crashing to the floor. I stood paralyzed by the shock of what seemed like an explosion. Even my grandfather, who had rushed up from downstairs to stop the fight, froze in his tracks when he saw my mother laying on the floor in a heap of upturned chairs and nightstands.

That was it. After all the previous arguments, this was the one event - just a few seconds of pain and anger and frustration exploding to the surface - that ended my parents relationship forever. Later that evening, on a rainy night in late December, my father walked out of their upstairs bedroom with a large suitcase in one hand and a black overcoat in the other. He came downstairs and stood for a minute in the front foyer. He looked around. He seemed to want to say something, but couldn't quite find the words.

My mother came out of the kitchen and stared at him, but didn't say a thing. My brother and I turned from the board game we had been playing and looked at the two just standing there. No one dared speak. Then my father simply turned and walked out the door. He got into our old Ford, started the engine, and drove away. He never looked back. My mother just stood there on the front porch looking up the road long after he had gone. Finally, with an air of deep resignation, she came back into the house and walked straight into the kitchen. That was the last time I ever saw my father.

That winter seemed especially cold. Winds from the north swept down the Great Plains and turned the flat grasslands of central Texas into a frozen wasteland. Walking to school each day seemed like a battle against bursts of wind that cut right through to your bones. At night, as I lay in my bed on the second floor of my grandparent's house, the walls and windows shrieked and whistled, and at times I could feel a draft of cool air pass over the two blankets I used for cover.

That winter stands out in my memory, not only for the bitter cold, but for the change that came over my mother in those months. After my father left she seemed to shrink and physically pull into herself. On many days she didn't even bother to change out of her pajamas and robe.

She stopped taking an interest in helping my younger brother get dressed and ready for school in the morning. After he left the house without his hat or mittens a couple of times, I took over the duties of making sure he was ready to walk out the door with everything he needed.

My mother began to drink, or, to be more accurate, she began to drink a lot more than she had before. My father and mother had always been drinkers, and looking back now, I'm convinced that their drinking, especially when they took it too far, added fuel to their fights. But on those occasions it was usually my father who drank to the point of passing out. My mother always seemed to be more in control of her drinking.

Once my father was gone, almost every afternoon, when we came in from school, she would have a drink in her hand, and more than once we came home to find her passed out on the couch. My grandfather tried to keep her away from the bottle, but all his efforts were in vain. He kept saying, "Giver her time. She'll come out of it." But she didn't. It got worse.

When Spring came we all hoped that the warmer temperatures and brighter days would help her feel better, but she continued to decline. Life, that bear we must wrestle against every day of our existence, had somehow defeated her, had knocked her down with a force ten times that of my father's fist, and she gave up trying to fight it. On a hot day in July my grandfather helped her into his pickup and drove her to a mental facility in Dallas.

Then, in September, just two months later, shortly after the beginning of the school year, my grandfather, out working in the fields on a hot afternoon, suffered a massive heart attack and collapsed. By the time my grandmother made it to him he was dead. For the first time in my life I experienced death in a very personal way.

I remember suffering deeply, feeling pain like I had never felt it before, but all the adults around me didn't have time for my emotions. They were all trying to figure out how to take care of the funeral, and figure out how to survive this catastrophe. I thought that my mother might come home for the funeral, but my grandmother explained that she was just too sick. The doctors felt that it wasn't a good idea for her to leave the hospital at that time.

Chapter 5

We Move to El Paso

Right after the funeral, my grandmother, my father's brother, and his wife, all with a somber countenance, and a look of utter resignation in the face of all the calamities that had befallen the family, gathered around the kitchen table and talked about what to do. The children all sat in the living room, uninterested in play, somehow understanding the momentousness nature of the conversation taking place in the adjoining room.

The adults all agreed that it was impossible to keep the farm. My uncle had never liked farming anyway. My grandmother reluctantly realized that she couldn't continue to take care of me and my brother, and made the decision to move into town. My aunt and uncle agreed to take care of us along with their own children.

A couple of weeks later my uncle drove to El Paso where he had been offered a job. After finding a place for us to live temporarily, he came back and loaded his wife, his two kids, my brother, and finally me, into the car. We then set off on the long drive over the desert to El Paso. Somewhere around Midland, Texas we stopped for the night at a ramshackle roadside motel. It was the first time I had ever stayed in a motel room. I can still remember lying in bed that night and hearing cars rush by on the highway, wondering where all those people could be going.

The other impression from that trip, which has stayed with me all these years, was how desolate the countryside was as we drove west toward El Paso. There were long stretches where we saw absolutely no indication of human habitation. For the first time in my life I became acutely aware that the western part of the United States was a vast open space, punctuated by small congregations of humans separated by huge distances. I remember thinking to myself that the world is so large and humans are so small. We exist on a gigantic planet that doesn't care, doesn't even notice the tiny humans running around like so many busy ants, living their trivial lives.

Those first few months in a new city weren't easy. My uncle talked about how nice it was in El Paso. "And you can find good jobs there," he insisted. But when we arrived at the house where we were to stay temporarily, which was the home of a friend of my uncle's, we realized that not everyone was doing equally well in this supposed paradise. The house was old and rundown, badly in need of painting. There was an old car without wheels, and on blocks, just to the left of the driveway.

As we pulled up in front of the house I asked my uncle, "are we going to live here?"

"Only for a short time, until we can get our own place. Don't worry," he said with a smile, "it will be fine."

I wasn't reassured. Everything looked so dilapidated. When we entered the house we were introduced to my uncle's friend. The first thing I noticed about him was that he needed a shave and looked like he had just been asleep. His wife, overweight and disheveled, and their two children, dirty and barely out of diapers, sat limply on a large grey couch in the living room. My first thought, as I surveyed the interior of this house, was let's get back in the car and return to the farm in Hamlin.

My uncle kept a stiff smile on his face as we talked about our trip. We discussed the drive, how many hours it took us to make our way here, and where we stopped for gas and for lodging. After a suitable time exchanging pleasantries, my uncle's friend led us through the house to a small, dirty room at the end of a long hallway. The room had one bed along the far wall opposite the door, and there were two small tables on each side of the bed. To the right side of the door was a single wooden chair that had seen better days and was in need of paint. This drab room served as our home for the next six months.

Since there was only one bed in the room, my aunt prepared a place for the kids to sleep on the floor along one of the walls. I remember that first night so vividly. I wanted to cry, but I wasn't sure exactly why. We were safe, and at least I was together with my brother and my cousins. And I looked forward to exploring this strange new city. I had never been in a city this large before, and was very curious to see what it was like. But being forced to sleep on the floor in this dingy room made me feel homesick for the farm, and for the life I had lived just a little more than a year earlier. For the first time I really felt that we were poor, and I wondered what sin we had committed to deserve everything that had happened to us over the last year.

At the end of the week my aunt took me to the local elementary school just a few blocks away from our temporary home. It was so big. I had never seen a school building so large, with so many children. I couldn't believe that there could possibly be that many kids in one city, but here they were. I was even more amazed when I was told that this was only one of a number of schools of equal or even larger size in the city.

After ascending a large set of stairs, and entering what looked to me to be these gigantic front doors, we were led to a busy office area. I was told to sit on a wooden bench while my aunt talked to the principle. As I sat there I watched a number of teachers and children scurrying in and out of the office and in the hallway in what seemed to me at the time a beehive of activity. I was then led down a long, wide hallway to a classroom. Entering the door of that classroom seemed like entering a foreign country. I tried to avoid eye contact with these strange kids, but I could feel them staring at me as the teacher showed me to my desk.

Over the next several months I obtained a completely new kind of education, one that had absolutely nothing to do with books or math problems. This new education consisted of the lessons learned when several boys decide to shove you into a locker simply because you happen to be the new kid. I was forced to learn very quickly the social skills necessary to get a group of girls to let you sit with them at lunch, or how to keep the bullies from targeting you on the playground.

In order to survive in this strange world I had to develop keen observational skills. This town, this school, and the people with whom I came in contact on a daily basis, were so different from those I had known in Hamlin. I had to learn to fit in and survive in this foreign environment, and the only way to do this was to become astute at observing the rituals and the practices of those around me.

I soon learned how to be a part of the group, and even though I quickly learned how to make my way in this new, strange world, I never completely fit in. I was an outsider. I was always a person who kept just a little distance from others in what seemed to me a very strange place.

I now realize that this experience, at such a young age, turned out to be a blessing in disguise. It's my strong conviction that artists must be somewhat estranged from the world around them. Artists have to be observers. On the one hand they must be able to empathize with the people they know and the environment they inhabit, but they must also have a certain distance as well. This allows them to develop the skills they need to objectively evaluate the society around them. Artists who fit in too comfortably in the world they know as children, who are seemingly well-adjusted, seem to have a difficult time seeing the unique strangeness of the culture and society they depict in their work, and thus have difficulty developing a truly original vision in their art.

That's one of the amazing things about living in a particular country or region, or existing as part of a certain culture. There must be thousands of micro-cultures in the world, all seemingly normal to the people who live in them. But really, if you look closely, all these little tribal groups maintain a set of characteristics that seem utterly bizarre to people who aren't a part of that particular tribe or group. I hadn't even moved out of the state of Texas, yet El Paso truly seemed like a different culture than the one I had inhabited in Hamlin. I had to find a way to understand this new cultural environment.

While I lived on the farm in Hamlin I never questioned why we did things a certain way, why we had certain attitudes and beliefs. This was just the way the world worked it seemed to me. Why should I question it? The social characteristics that my family and I took for granted seemed pre-ordained, and I'm sure that, at the time, I thought that the rest of the world must work exactly the same way.

When I was pulled abruptly from that world, that lovely existence I loved so much, I quickly learned that other places weren't the same. At the tender age of eleven I became a sociologist, a psychologist, and maybe a little bit of a philosopher. And those observational skills, although I never suspected it at the time, became the basis of what I would need to become an artist years later.

I find it so funny. Our art schools teach all kinds of mechanical skills - how to draw, how to create perspective, how to mix colors. That all seems so secondary to me, almost beside the point. What an artist really must learn is how to obtain a certain amount of philosophical perspective, how to gain a degree of distance, even a certain alienation from the society they inhabit. Art schools rarely teach anything like that.

I often wonder how many young people would want to be artists if they knew the simple fact that, in order to be a truly great and an original artist, they had to alienate themselves from the world around them. If they were told that they might be forced to risk the anger and rejection of even their family and close friends, who are more than comfortable with the way things are in their small and insular world, how many would sign up for the job. All the glamour that comes along with being an artist is more than counteracted by the alienation inherent in the creative process, since being creative means exposing the blind spots of the society the artist inhabits.

For me, the price of becoming an artist is isolation and rejection from my family and my friends. There are so very few that understand what it means to be an artist. I've spent my entire life as an outsider, living in a world totally incomprehensible even to my own children and grandchildren. That is the price paid for being an artist.

As I was saying before my rather lengthy digression, I began to see the world so differently living in El Paso. This very unique spot on the globe, as every place is in its own way, was a perfect place to get to know the wider world. I learned that there were very distinct classes in this city. We Americans tend to ignore class differences, and assume that in the United States class divisions don't really exist. The strata of class only exists in Europe we so naively tell ourselves.

But life in El Paso provided ample proof that class not only exists in America, it is an essential building block of life in this country. In El Paso, there seemed to me to be three very distinct classes. The lowest echelon were the Mexicans and the blacks who worked in the least desirable jobs, if they had jobs at all. The children of these families were despised by all the white kids in the school. Even the teachers, all white of course, didn't treat them any better than the kids did. If a white kid and a Mexican kid got into a fight, you could rest assured that the Mexican child would be expelled, and the white kid would escape punishment. In fact, most of the time the white kid would almost be seen as heroic.

The highest class in my school consisted of the children of the rich families, the kids whose fathers were doctors, or lawyers, or business owners. The children from these families learned very quickly that they inhabited a world of special privilege, and thus assumed an air of superiority with everyone else that they, from their lofty perch, considered below them in status. I learned this by the end of the first week.

The class in the middle, uneasily wedged between the rich kids on the one hand, and the poor Mexicans and blacks on the other, was the class I now occupied. It was made up of the children of truck drivers, gas station attendants, shop keepers, and other working class families. Of course, we resented being excluded from the company of the rich kids, but we thanked our lucky stars that we weren't grouped with the poor Mexican and black kids.

As I became more familiar with the social dynamics in my school, and observed the interactions - or lack of interactions - between the social strata of the community at large, what struck me the most was the fact that everyone, no matter what group they were cast into, accepted this social hierarchy without question. Or, if they did question it, they seemed unable, or unwilling, to see a way of changing the conditions before them. I kept asking myself why things had to be organized in this particular way. Who made these rules, and who declared that rich kids couldn't possibly be friends with poor children, or that white kids couldn't associate with black children.

At the time, I didn't understand how this was changing the way I approached the world. Now, I can clearly see that my feelings of alienation from the social structure of my school and town sparked the formation of a perspective that would lead me to take a certain direction in my art more than two decade later.

Around the end of the school year, four or five months after we arrived in El Paso, my uncle finally found a house for us. During a July heat wave, we moved into a small, two-bedroom house of our own on a quiet street a dozen blocks or so from where I went to school. The house was cramped and a little rundown, but I liked it. It was such a relief to have our own place again.

Since I was older than the other kids, and was soon to be a teenager, my aunt and uncle decided to give me my own room. Even though there were only two bedrooms in this house, there was a small room in the back of the house that was reconfigured into a bedroom for me. I loved this small room. It was the first space that I could call my own, and I was soon decorating it with little mementos that I collected. But this room later became the scene of one of the most horrible experiences of my life.

Chapter 6

The World War II Years

Soon things in El Paso began to feel fairly normal. I was beginning to find my way around the neighborhood, I had made several friends, and my aunt and uncle seemed happy and content with our new life. In September, I went back to school and settled into my classes. I was beginning to enjoy going to school again, as I had in Hamlin. Then, suddenly, on a cool December day, events in the outside world changed everything.

I can still remember walking into the living room and seeing my aunt and uncle sitting on the couch, listening to the radio. Both stared forward, with long, drawn faces. A man was talking rapidly among bleeps of hissing and static. Much of what he was saying I couldn't understand. But I kept hearing Pearl Harbor, Pearl Harbor, Pearl Harbor, over and over again.

"What is Pearl Harbor?" I asked.

"It's a place in Hawaii," my aunt replied solemnly.

"What's going on?" I asked after another minute or two.

At first they didn't reply, they just kept staring at the radio. Finally, my uncle said, "We've been attacked. The Japanese have attacked us. We are at war."

It's interesting how children interpret world events like this. I had heard of Hawaii, and I knew that somewhere way out there, over the ocean, you would come to a group of islands known as Hawaii. I also knew that the Japanese were the people who lived on islands on the other side of the Pacific Ocean. I had learned all this in one of my classes at some point in my few years of education. I also understood what war was, and how awful it could be for the soldiers who were forced to fight.

Yet, it all seemed so remote to my naive eleven year old imagination. War was something that took place in some distant foreign land, and people who fought in wars were from other countries thousands of mile away. Surely, something that happened, however disastrous, in a place called Pearl Harbor, wouldn't affect me or my family. Our only connection to all these events would be the radio reports that my aunt and uncle were so intent on listening to for what seemed like hours.

It didn't take long for me to realize that this war was something that touched everyone, and would change everything in our lives. Within weeks I started seeing men in uniform. Up and down the street where we lived men began to leave their homes and join the service.

Things also changed in my family. My aunt and uncle seemed to loose the carefree quality that I had come to expect from them before the start of the war. They always looked solemn and troubled. My uncle, who could be very funny when he was in a good mood, seemed to never want to crack a joke now. On several occasions over the winter I overheard my aunt and uncle talking in hushed whispers about something that was obviously very contentious.

I soon learned what they were arguing about. My uncle had decided to enlist rather than wait to be drafted. My aunt didn't want him to go and was very upset about it, but how could my uncle resist the pressure to serve when every able-bodied man in the city was signing up. In the summer of 1942 he packed a small suitcase, said goodby, and walked to the train station to report for duty.

A couple of months later my aunt took a job with the local Red Cross offices in town. She said that she felt it was her duty to help the war effort. Both my brother and I helped by participating in the school's periodic scrap drives. We wanted to play our part as well.

After my uncle left for the service, and my aunt went to work, we settled into a routine that lasted most of the next three years. My brother and I went to school each day, our aunt went to her job. Each night we listened to the radio to hear news of the war. Once a week we walked to the local movie theater. I didn't like watching the newsreels that always presented updates on the progress of the war, but I never said anything about it to my aunt. She always watched them with an intense interest, hoping that it might give her some idea about what her husband might be doing.

At first he was stationed in various camps in the United States. He told us, in the weekly letters that we received, that he was going through training and, for the most part, it was very easy. He kept repeating that we had nothing to worry about, that the training wasn't that difficult, and the hardest thing for him was the boredom of guard duty.

Early in 1944 he was sent to Australia, and I could tell that my aunt began to worry more. The news from the Pacific was of the terrible battles for various islands, and she wondered if he was involved. Now, when we watched the newsreels, and they showed action in the South Pacific, she could hardly bare to watch, and she often had tears in her eyes.

Apparently, he had been involved in several of the assaults on Pacific islands, but the letters kept coming, and he kept saying that he was fine and not to worry. He kept telling us that he was safe, and was enjoying the tropical climate.

The last year of the war coincided with my first year in high school. By March of 1945, as I was finishing my freshman year classes, almost everyone was talking about the war winding down in Europe. According to the newsreels, American forces were advancing rapidly across Germany, and everyone was hopeful that the war would soon be over.

Since my uncle had been safe for almost three years now, I thought surely nothing would happen, but on a warm Friday afternoon in April, when I arrived home from school, I found my aunt sitting at the kitchen table crying. I knew immediately that something had happened to my uncle.

I yanked the telegram out of my aunt's hand and read the short note. He was wounded, and was on a hospital ship heading home. Once the ship arrived we would be informed of his condition. We later learned that he had been wounded during the battle for the island of Okinawa, one of the worst and most costly battles in American history.

His company, one of the first to hit the beaches, was immediately pinned down and unable to advance off the shore. In the first hour more than a third of his company was killed. My uncle was one of the lucky ones. After he was wounded he lay on the beach for hours, but was eventually rescued and loaded on a boat that transported him to a hospital ship.

"At least he's alive. At least he's alive," my aunt kept repeating. "He'll be ok, I'm sure of it."

I wasn't so sure. I had seen too many men come back from the war with terrible wounds, missing arms or legs, sitting in wheelchairs, staring into empty space. When I saw these men, I always felt that my family was so much luckier. Now, I realized that we were just like them.

My aunt brought my uncle home on a warm summer day in August of 1945. She helped him out of the car and into his wheelchair as his kids, and my brother and I, stood by the car and watched. We didn't know what to say, but once he was properly positioned in the wheelchair he looked up at us and smiled. "Don't worry," he said, "I'm on the mend. I'll be like new in no time."

He was clearly in pain. I noticed immediately that he had lost a lot of weight, and was probably forty or fifty pounds lighter than when we saw him late in 1943. That last visit was when he was on leave over the Christmas holidays and getting ready to ship oversees. As he sat in his wheelchair, I studied his features and could see that his cheeks were deeply sunken, but he seemed in good spirits. We all breathed a sigh of relief.

By the time I returned to school in the fall he was already much better. He had suffered bullet and shrapnel wounds to the leg and stomach. We worried most about the stomach wound, but actually that healed over time and didn't present long term problems for him. His leg wounds were more problematic. The doctor said that his knee on his right leg was shattered and would probably never function properly again. The prognosis was that, with a little time, he would be able to walk fairly normally and with only a pronounced limp.

By the middle of November he was already showing signs of rapid improvement, and was using crutches to get around the house. By Christmas, he switched to a cane, and was already making his way down the street to his favorite bar. He liked going to this bar on an almost daily basis since everyone there treated him with the respect of a war hero. His limp was becoming a badge of honor.

At this point in the story Emma stopped and suggested that we should take a break. It was getting late, and the restaurant was about to close. I agreed, but I told her that I was fascinated by her story and wanted to hear the rest. "We haven't even arrived at your early years as an artist. I can't wait to hear about how you went from a childhood in Texas to the life of such a talented artist."

She laughed. "Well, I can tell you about how I became an artist, but I can't claim that I have any talent."

"Well I can," I replied. "I can't wait to hear more."

"Well," she said, "I'm not at all sure that my life will prove all that interesting, but I'm willing to tell you more tomorrow."

After paying the bill I walked her back to her hotel and talked to her about our plans for the next day. "Listen," I began. "Let's meet tomorrow at my apartment. I really want to hear the rest of your story. I will completely clear my schedule, and we can spend the entire day together."

"That sounds very nice," she replied. "I would like that. I hope my story lives up to your expectations."

"Oh, don't worry about that," I said. "I look forward to it." And on that note she entered the hotel.

Chapter 7

The Trials of a Teenage Girl

Promptly at 10 a.m. the next morning Emma arrived at my apartment. After greetings and preparation of coffee and a few snacks, we sat down in my living room. I asked her how she slept and if her hotel room was adequate. She replied that she was happy with everything and that she slept quite well. "But I'm worried," she continued, "I'm worried that I'm boring you with the story of my life. Just tell me if you don't want to hear any more. The important thing is that, after many years of struggle I became an artist and have worked on developing my craft ever since. Maybe that's all you need to know."

"No, no," I replied. "Please don't think for a minute that I'm not very curious to hear more. What you've told me so far is absolutely fascinating, and I can't wait to hear more. Being a New York girl, life in Texas seems totally strange and exotic. I have to say that Texas seems almost like a foreign country to me. In fact, I now think that hearing the story of someone growing up in Europe would seem less strange. I had never thought about how different life in the west is from what we in the east have experienced. Up until now I believed that when someone said that they are an American I've just assumed that they share a similar story to my own. You're making me realize just how different the western regions of the United States are."

She laughed. "Yes, I guess the experience of growing up in Texas must seem totally bizarre to a New Yorker. Since I once lived in this great city, so different from rural ways, I can see that myself."

At this point she paused and looked down. With slightly trembling hands she removed a loose thread from her skirt. I could tell that something very troubling was bothering her. "I do want to continue to tell you my story if you want to hear more, but in order to proceed in a way that would make my life make sense, I have to tell you about something that happened to me that was truly awful, something that completely altered the course of my story forever, and something that I've never told anyone else. In fact, I can't believe I'm even contemplating telling it to you now."

She looked up at me with eyes just beginning to fill with tears. "I don't even know if I'll be able to tell you without breaking down, but if I don't tell you about this awful incident the rest of my life story will probably remain very confusing. Frankly, I'm not sure you would understand what happened later in my life."

I paused for a minute, and wasn't sure how to respond to this, and I wasn't really sure how to make her feel comfortable telling me. At the same time, if she didn't want to tell me, I wanted her to feel comfortable with that decision as well.

"Listen," I began, "I understand that you're giving me an account of things that are deeply personal. If there is anything that you don't want to tell me that's fine. I completely understand. I can well imagine that some things could be very hard to talk about. That's also very understandable. But I feel that over the short time that we've known each other we really have developed a remarkably close friendship."

"Yes," she replied, "I feel the same way."

""We do have a professional relationship," I commented, "and that's how we got to know one another. But I think our relationship has moved well beyond something based on a professional connection. I think we really related to each other from the very beginning. In many ways I think we understand each other. We've both had to make it in an art world that is also a man's world.

"So let me say, as a friend, that I want you to be able to talk to me about anything. You can count on me always being a friend that will empathize and support you. Forget our professional connection," I said with a swift wave of the hand. "I want to be a friend in every way, and I would be honored to feel that you can trust me, and know that I will never betray your trust."

She paused and gathered her thoughts. "Well, okay, I'll give it a try. Just keep in mind that this next chapter in my story is going to be very hard to tell. I might get more than a little emotional at times. I just hope I can get through it." And with that she resumed her story. What she told me was worse than I ever imagined.

In February of 1946, not even a year since my uncle had returned from the war, we got word that my grandmother, still living in Hamlin, had developed a bad case of pneumonia, and was suffering from some serious heart problems. My aunt decided that she should spend some time nursing her and, hopefully, helping her to recover. My uncle, largely recovered from his war wounds, said that he could take care of the kids while she was gone.

The very night we dropped my aunt at the train station I helped my brother get ready for bed, made sure he was asleep, and then got ready for bed myself. Shortly after 10 pm I was settled into bed and was falling asleep when I heard the door to my room open slightly. I thought my uncle was just checking to make sure I was asleep. Then I heard him move quietly across the room and stop at my bedside. I turned slightly and looked up at him in the dark.

"Don't worry," he said, "it's just me."

I couldn't understand why he had come into my room. Then he lifted the covers and climbed into bed beside me. I could feel my body tighten, but I wasn't sure why. I just felt very uneasy. Somehow I sensed that something was wrong, but I wasn't sure why I should be afraid.

He moved closer and then put his arm over me. I held my breath and lay perfectly still. I didn't know what to do or how to react. After a minute or so he said, "just relax. Everything is fine." Then, all of a sudden, he got on top of me. His full weight pushed me deep into the mattress. He seemed so heavy. I struggled to say something, but nothing came out of my mouth. I tried to push him away, but he caught my arm and twisted it back. The force of his grip hurt and I moaned.

"Keep your voice down! I don't want you to wake up your brother," he whispered.

"Please, no," I cried. He then put his hand over my mouth to keep me from screaming.

All of a sudden there was this searing pain deep in my gut. I felt like he was cutting me open, and I thought it would go on forever. After what seemed like an eternity he finally stopped. He was so heavy I could hardly breath. Then he rolled over, got up, and walked out of the room like nothing had happened.

The next day I did everything I could to avoid him. I was afraid to be in the same room with him. But he was always there. He constantly stared at me during dinner and made a point of standing in the door of the kitchen watching me while I was rinsing the dishes.

That night I couldn't sleep. I was so worried that he would come in again. The second night was no better. I kept asking myself what I could do. If I left and ran away where would I go, and what would happen to my brother? If I stayed, how could I endure being around him.

After several more nights I thought that he had decided to leave me alone, and I began to be able to sleep fitfully. But then it happened again. As soon as he entered the room I jumped up and tried to run for the door, but he grabbed me around the neck, choking me with his arm. There was nothing I could do to stop him.

After the second time I thought he would wait several more days to come in, but the very next night the door opened again and he was on top of me before I could react. But this time I was on the edge of the bed, and was able to shove him aside just enough that he fell to one side. I ran for the bedroom door. Just a few seconds later I made it out the front door of the house and into the middle of the street, running for my life. I ran for probably eight or nine blocks without letting up for a second. I was barefoot and my feet were hurting. At one point, when I felt I was far enough away from the house, I looked down at my feet. They were bleeding, but I was afraid he would come looking for me, so I kept going.

Finally, I came to a police station and ran in, crying furiously, unable to speak. A police officer sat at a high counter. I ran up to the counter and then just crumbled to the floor. He came out from around the barrier and knelt down beside me, asking me what was wrong, but I couldn't speak. I just kept sobbing. He soon led me down a long hallway and into a room with a single table and four chairs. Another police officer brought a glass of water and placed it on the table in front of me. My first words were, "please save me."

For the next two hours I sat in that dingy room and told the police officer what had happened while he took notes on a yellow lined pad of paper. I remember how big he seemed, sitting very upright with large rounded shoulders. His uniform was dark blue with light blue trim, a name tag hung over a shirt pocket, and one arm was covered with gold strips. After a while I couldn't cry anymore. It was like all my tears were gone. I was still in my nightgown, but they gave me a blanket to put over my shoulders.

After I had given my statement, the officer told me that they couldn't pursue the situation until the morning and that I should try to rest. The only place they had for me to sleep was a jail cell. He took me to the back of the station and ushered me into one of the cells. "You can sleep here for the rest of night," he said. Although I had been the victim I felt like I deserved to be in a jail cell. I felt dirty, and I wondered if the police officers thought the same thing.

The next morning they brought my uncle into the station. From a back room I could just see him through a crack in the door, talking to the officers. He said that I was totally hysterical and couldn't be trusted. "She's been acting very strangely lately."

"But did you have sex with her last night, or any other night?" the officer asked.

"No, absolutely not, sir," my uncle stated emphatically.

"She says you did," the officer replied.

"Look," my uncle stated, and pulled up his pants leg to show the gruesome scars from his wounds. "I can hardly walk. I have a bad limp. I couldn't have forced her to have sex with me if I had tried."

The two police officers paused. This clearly caused them to rethink the situation. After a few minutes they escorted him down the hall and placed him in an interrogation room. They made me sit in another room for more than two hours. As I sat there, I started thinking that they were going to believe him and make me go back. I wanted to cry again, but couldn't find a way to let the tears come out.

Finally, one of the officers entered the room and sat down at the table across from me. He looked very grim. "Given the situation," he began, in a neutral, official tone, "we don't have enough evidence to hold your uncle. He says he didn't do anything, and that you have been acting strangely the past week or two. He thinks you might be having trouble in school, and that's what's causing all this. He couldn't understand why you would, all of a sudden, without any warning, run to the police station. Have you been having trouble in school?"

"No," I replied meekly.

He paused and looked at me. I kept my head down and stared at the table. I was afraid to make eye contact.

He dropped his pen on the yellow pad in front of him and leaned forward toward me, resting his elbows on the table. "Would you like to go back home and try to work things out with your uncle? It might be the best thing to do."

"No, please no," I cried. The tears started again. "I can't go back. He will hurt me. I'm begging you, please don't make me go back."

The officer coughed, cleared his throat, and then leaned back in his chair, as if to indicate that there wasn't much more he could do. "If you won't go back we will have no choice but to send you to a foster home, a home for abandoned children, and once you're there you won't be able to leave. You won't be able to change your mind. Are you sure that's what you want to do?"

I sat there for several minutes trying to understand. I didn't really know what foster homes were like. Of course, I had heard of them, and they sounded like awful places where poor and lonely children were sent. The way the police officer made it sound was not reassuring.

"Couldn't I go somewhere else," I asked tentatively. "Maybe I could go back to Hamlin and stay with my grandmother.

"No," came the emphatic reply. "We asked your uncle about other relatives that could take you in. He said that your mother is in a hospital for the insane, and your grandmother is too sick to take care of you. He told us that she probably won't live much longer. Going to live with other relatives is out of the question. You must make a choice right now. Go back home and work things out with your uncle, or we will place you in the custody of a foster program."

With a trembling voice I said, "send me to the foster home."

Chapter 8

Life as an Orphan

A few hours later a police officer walked into the room, told me to follow him, and then escorted me to his police car. He opened the back door and told me to get in. I felt like I was being taken to prison.

But the foster home wasn't that bad. Yes, conditions were spartan. I lived in a long room with eight beds lined up against the wall. There was only one window at the far end of the room, so it always seemed dark and dreary, even on a sunny day. Each girl was given a large wooden box which just fit under the bed. All our personal possessions had to fit in that one box.

The rest of the facility was equally drab and shabby. In the common area, where most of the girls gathered in the evening after dinner, was a brown couch with sagging cushions, a few wooden chairs, and three small desks with graffiti scratched into the wooden surface. We were told that the desks were reserved for girls working on school homework. The dining hall consisted of several rickety tables placed end to end, with a dirty swinging door leading into the kitchen.

The home imposed very strict procedures. The staff rang the bell every morning at 6 a.m. At 6:30 a.m. we were expected to be fully dressed and in line for breakfast in the dining hall. Most of us, still half asleep, ate our meager breakfast in silence. At 7 a.m. the bus departed for school. In the evening, dinner was always served at 6 p.m. After dinner, we were assigned various clean-up responsibilities. Those chores usually took about an hour. Then, most of us worked on homework until it was time to get ready for bed. The staff ran checks to make sure each one of us was in our room at 8: 55 p.m. Lights were turned off promptly at 9 p.m.

Most of the girls followed the rules and didn't make trouble. There was little to gain by causing problems. Most of these girls, just like me, came from very traumatic experiences, and although no one really liked being in this place, most of us accepted it as far better and more stable than what we had experienced on the outside.

There were occasional breakdowns. On numerous nights I could hear a girl crying in bed. This happened the most with the girls who were new to the home. Occasionally, one of the girls would break down over some incident. One girl cut her wrists in the bathroom one night. On another occasion a girl, who had been simply sitting in the common area, suddenly got up, walked over to a wall and started slamming her head into it. Several of us grabbed her and pulled her down to the floor, holding her still until the staff took over. Soon an ambulance came and took her away. We never saw her again. But these incidents were fairly rare, punctuating a rather dull and monotonous routine that prevailed most of the time.

One day, after I had been at the foster home for about a year, I was called to the office. Being summoned to the front of the building, where the office was located, was very unusual. I don't think that I had been there more than five or six times the whole year that I had lived at the home.

Apparently, a couple by the name of John and Edith Isenhath wanted to meet me. The head of the facility, Miss Johnson, called me into her office. She was a large women, always attired in a dress that seemed a little too small for her big boned structure. She explained to me that the Isenhaths wanted to adopt a girl, and on a visit a few days earlier, had noticed me in the common area. They wanted to set up an interview to see if I was acceptable.

When she was ready to conclude the short interview she got up from her chair, walked around her desk to the side where I sat, and looked at me with a concentrated focus. After a short pause, to make sure I was listening, she stated in an emphatic tone, "Be on your best behavior, and maybe, if you're lucky, you might just get out of here."

The next day one of the workers at the facility drove me to a large church for the interview. As I was to find out later, the Isenhaths were devoted members of the Methodist Church, and the building I now found myself walking into was the largest for that denomination in El Paso. The Isenhath's primary interest in adopting a girl from the foster home came from a sermon given by the church's minister.

A few weeks earlier I had seen this minister, dressed in a fancy dark suit and slick dress shoes, polished to a glossy shine, walking around the building. As he made small talk with several of the girls, I was struck by his large smile that seemed permanently plastered to his face. After his visit, he felt motivated to encourage members of his congregation to reach out to "these poor girls" and consider adoption.

Despite the good intentions of the Isenhaths, my guess is that, of all the couples in that congregation that might have adopted a teenage girl, they were the least prepared. Edith had suffered an injury in early adulthood, and was told she couldn't have children. It was probably for the best anyway. Her husband was very regimented in his daily routine and didn't like the carefree way of children. His habits were well established at the beginning of their marriage, and he tolerated no deviation. Edith adapted to his routines and the demands he placed on her, and over time she learned to follow his commands without question. For her, his comfort became her only priority.

Once we arrived, I was led into a large community room at the back of the church where both John and Edith sat. They were sitting at a table in the middle of the room. The first thing I noticed about them was their perfect posture. Both sat forward in their chairs looking rigid and uncomfortable. John was dressed in a brown suit and black tie. The suit seemed very stiff and a little out of date. He was partially bald, with short clipped hair, and he wore wire-rimmed glasses. Edith wore a conservative dress in an unassuming grey color. I could see no jewelry other than her wedding ring, and her hair was pulled back in a tight bun.

The staff member from the orphanage led me across the room, and I was invited to sit down at the table opposite the Isenhaths. There was a moment of uneasy silence. Then, all of a sudden, Mr. Isenhath blurted out his first question, "How are your grades?"

I was somewhat startled by this sudden outburst. This question seemed like an odd place to start a conversation, but I quickly gained my composure and answered, "I am a strait A student."

He seemed somewhat surprised by my quick response, and after another minute he replied, "Well, that's good to hear."

Edith now jumped in and took a milder, friendlier tone. "What are your favorite subjects in school?"

"I like English and biology," I began. "History is interesting at times. I'm not as interested in home economics, but, I guess, we learn useful things that I'll be able to use in the future."

"Yes, I would think so," Edith replied.

Mr. Isenhath jumped in again in the same blunt manner. Not one for any kind of conversational transition, he came right to the point of the meeting. "Would you like for us to adopt you?"

Edith jumped in before I could reply, "John, give her a minute to let her get to know us. We just met."

Although admonished he wasn't willing to give up much ground. "Well, I don't want to sit here and waste my time if she isn't interested."

Another uncomfortable moment of silence ensued. I really didn't know what to say, and I was worried about disappointing Miss Johnson. She had been so pointed in her instructions, and she clearly wanted me to make a good impression. It seemed that Mr. Isenhath didn't really like me, and I didn't have the slightest idea how to make him change his mind. I finally decided to try to do the best I could to convince him that I really was a nice person. "If you would be willing to give me a chance I would like to try it," I said hesitantly.

Edith leaned forward. "Oh that's nice dear. I'm sure everything would work out very well. We have a nice house, and you could have your own bedroom. I think you would like it."

"You will have to follow our rules," Mr. Isenhath stated emphatically. "I won't tolerate inappropriate behavior under any circumstances. We live a simple life, and I won't put up with any shenanigans." He adjusted his position into an even tighter posture than the one he had maintained for the length of the interview. "I know that girls in foster homes come from bad families. That kind of behavior won't be acceptable in our home. Do I make myself clear?"

"Yes sir," I replied meekly.

Another awkward moment of silence. Then, with no warning, Mr. Isenhath stood up and announced, "I think we're done here. Edith, let's talk to Miss Johnson."

I stood up quickly and reached out to shake hands. Mr. Isenhath grabbed my hand and gave it two swift jerks up and down. He then pivoted away. They left the room quickly without looking back. I just stood there awkwardly not knowing what to do. Finally, the person who had brought me came back into the room and told me that we could go now. He then escorted me back to the car.

I had no idea at that point if they wanted to adopt me or not. Not a word was said to me about the interview or the adoption. Then, three days after my talk with the Isenhaths, and shortly after the bus had dropped us off from school, Miss Johnson pulled me aside and said, "Gather your things. The Isenhaths will be here in an hour to pick you up. They have adopted you." She started to walk away, but then remembered one last detail. "Oh, and by the way, your new name is Emma Isenhath."

When they arrived Miss Johnson escorted me out to the foyer where the Isenhaths waited. In order to break the ice Miss Johnson began, "Here she is, ready to go."

I thought I should say something so I whispered, "Hello, good to see you."

"Hello dear," Edith replied. Mr. Isenhath just stood there and stared at me. Within a couple of minutes my few things were placed in the trunk of the car, and I was told to get into the back seat. As we drove away I looked back at the foster home and wondered if my life with the Isenhaths would be any better than my existence at the orphanage.

As it turned out, my short time with the Isenhaths wasn't that unpleasant. I quickly adapted to their rituals, although they were very restrictive, and often very arbitrary. I learned to say as little as possible. If I talked about something too much, or got excited about something, Mr. Isenhath would soon get impatient and even angry. An animated teenage girl was the last thing he wanted to hear. Edith was a little easier to talk to, but she also had her limits. It became very obvious that they preferred a quiet and peaceful house, especially in the evening after dinner. Any display of emotion or excitement was totally out of the question.

I quickly realized that it was best to stay as restrained as possible during dinner, answer any questions with short, polite responses, and make sure that I always observed proper table manners. After dinner I found it best to spend most of the evening in my room working on my homework. If I got tired of my room, the best thing to do was to stay clear of Mr. Isenhath, He could become very cranky if I came into the living room and started talking to Edith.

If I had been forced to live with them longer I might have found this existence harder to accept. But they adopted me late in my junior year in high school, so I only spent the remainder of that year, and my senior year in their house.

Early in my senior year one of the guidance councilors, Mrs. Harding, called me into her office and talked to me about my future plans. She asked me what I had in mind after graduation. At that point I hadn't thought that much about it. I told her that I had been afraid to even bring the subject up with the Isenhaths.

"I don't understand why they wouldn't be willing to talk to you about what you plan to do after high school," she replied.

"I'm adopted," I said. She paused, looked me over like she was trying to figure out what that must be like, started to say something, but then stopped herself. She then seemed to gather her thoughts and came back to the point of why she called me into her office in the first place.

"Have you considered going to college? Your grades are very good. The quality of your writing is excellent. I really think you should consider applying for a scholarship. Do you think you could discuss the possibility of college with your parents?"

I didn't know how they would react to a request to go to college, and I was afraid to ask. But Mrs. Harding really encouraged me to consider it, and the more I thought about it the more the possibility really excited me. But how to approach the situation with the Isenhaths remained an enigma. I finally decided that I would send in the application and see if I got a scholarship. After all, I reasoned, I might be turned down. If that happened then talking with them would be beside the point. If I did succeed in acquiring a scholarship I could bring it up with them at that time.

About three months later Mrs. Harding pulled me out of class one day and told me the good news. I had a full scholarship to Smith College in Massachusetts. She was so excited. "Emma, do you know what this means? This is one of the best women's colleges in the country. This is a very hard school to get into. They admit only a fraction of the girls who apply. You not only got in, you got a full scholarship."

I couldn't believe what I was hearing. It was absolutely amazing, and I couldn't wait to tell the Isenhaths. Surely, they would think a scholarship like this a great opportunity. All the way home that day on the school bus I almost couldn't contain my excitement. One of my girlfriends said that she had never seen me so giddy, and she was probably right. I don't think I had ever been quite so thrilled with anything in my life. When Mr. Isenhath got home from work I grabbed Edith from the kitchen and asked her to come into the living room where Mr. Isenhath sat reading the newspaper.

"I have a scholarship to Smith College in Massachusetts," I blurted out, unable to hold back for one minute more. "Mrs. Harding says its one of the best colleges in the country. Can I go? I really want to go."

"Now wait a minute young lady," Mr. Isenhath commanded. "Let's just sit down and talk about this." Edith and I both took a seat. She chose a seat close to him on the couch, I sat in a chair across the room. "Where did you get the bright idea to apply to some college in Massachusetts. Do you realize how far away that is?"

"Mrs. Harding suggested I apply. She told me I have excellent grades and that I should go to a good college like Smith. So I applied. I didn't mention it to you because I wasn't sure they would accept me. Mrs. Harding said it's a very hard school to get into. She said they turn down most applicants. But I was accepted. In fact, I not only got in, I got a full scholarship. All my tuition is paid for by the college."

"Are they going to cover all your other expenses as well," Mr. Isenhath retorted. "You would have to travel all the way to Massachusetts. Do you know how much money it would cost to make such a trip. Then, who's going to look after you up there. Girls like you are liable to get into big trouble so far away from home and in a place like that. I've heard about what goes on at those colleges up there, and it isn't something we can even talk about in polite society. Can't you go to a college around here. Just because those people up there think their college is so grand doesn't mean they will give you an education any better than what you could get down here."

In a matter of one minute I went from a feeling of total elation to utter desolation. I sat there totally deflated, not knowing what to say. I looked at Edith, hoping she would take my side. Surely, she could find the courage to support me, but she just studied the dust on the coffee table in front of her. I went to bed that night and cried myself to sleep. I wondered if he would let me go to college at all.

Although Edith failed to support me in that initial conversation, at church the following Sunday she asked the minister if he knew of a college that would be good for me, something that would suit the needs of a young girl like me. He immediately told her about McMurry College in Abilene, Texas.

"McMurry is a fine Methodist College," he stated. "It's a small school, which is perfect for her. You know, kids, especially girls, can get lost at a large, secular university. These schools rarely provide religious guidance for young people. That's not the case at McMurry. They have small classes, require attendance at church every Wednesday night and Sunday morning, and they provide good Christian counseling. Yes, McMurry would be perfect for her, and I think I can get her a scholarship. With her good grades I'm sure they would be happy to have her. You can rest assured that she will get a good, solid Christian education."

The place sounded absolutely awful to me, but I kept my mouth shut. What good would it do to voice an opinion anyway?

About a month later, after church, the minister caught the three of us as we were leaving. He was very excited and clearly couldn't wait to pass on his news. There, on the front steps of the church, he told us that he had just received word that I had a full scholarship to McMurry. I remember standing there in the hot sun and simply wishing to go home. I wasn't at all happy with the thought of going to some small church school after being tempted with a place like Smith, but I thought that, at the very least, I would be able to go to college somewhere. Since it was in Abilene, I would be close to where I had lived until I was eleven. I might even be able to see my grandmother occasionally.

Since the minister had set this up, the Isenhaths couldn't say no. After some discussion of the situation when we got home from church, they agreed to provide me with the necessary funds to pay all expenses not covered by the scholarship. I don't think Mr. Isenhath liked it, since he was so tight with every penny that crossed his palm, but he felt obligated, especially given the fact that the minister had gone to so much trouble to work this out.

After my senior year ended I spent the summer largely alone and isolated. When Edith went into town on errands I asked her to drop me off at the public library. I then checked out as many books as the librarian allowed. When we returned home, I would go up to my room, shut the door, and read. By the end of the summer I must have made my way through at least sixty or seventy books.

Of course, as the summer went by, and I isolated myself more and more, the Isenhaths began to wonder what was wrong with me. To them, reading all the time was simply strange and unhealthy. Soon they were trying to get me out of my room and doing something "useful." Of course, that just made me all the more determined to resist their efforts. By the time I left for college in September of 1948, both of them had come to the conclusion that I was clearly damaged beyond redemption by whatever had happened to me before I had come to live with them. But they went through the motions of being the supportive parents. They wished me well at the bus station, and they said that if I needed anything that I should just call.

Chapter 9

College Life and My First Boyfriend

My first reaction when I reached McMurry was how small and desolate this supposed institution of higher learning was. I had always imagined that colleges were large, sprawling campuses with huge ivy covered buildings dedicated to learning at the highest level. McMurry was anything but sprawling. There were the usual buildings that had been designed to look "academic," but with the dry desert heat of Abilene, Texas, there certainly were no ivy vines climbing up the side of these buildings. In fact, the entire campus seemed bland and even a little rundown. The thought went through my head that why would anyone try to establish an institution of higher learning in the middle of the Texas prairie, in a drab, wind-blown town like Abilene.

The dorms were unadorned rust-colored brick buildings with no ornament. They were the height, if height is the appropriate word, of utilitarian construction meant to house students as efficiently as possible. They looked like overgrown rectangular boxes. In the middle of the extended stretch of facade was a small opening that served as an entrance. The hallways were long, airless corridors with dull brown floors and dirty beige walls.

The dorm rooms were all uniformly spartan. They consisted of a shallow wardrobe to the right and left as you entered, and two narrow beds on each wall. Under the window, caked with dust, was a small desk. The girls forced to live in this drab building tried to decorate their spaces with various items that added color, but it was largely a lost cause. In the end the rooms still seemed barren and lifeless.

As I began my Freshman semester I had hoped that my college courses would be more interesting than those in high school, but the level of academic excitement in this small college was only a marginal gain over what had been available in my high school. I was often bored by the content, and I thought that most of the professors weren't really that interested in inspiring the dull farm kids who represented the majority of students in their classes. Many of these so called scholars, who taught our classes, were really only glorified farm boys themselves.

In February of my freshman year, shortly after my second semester began, I met a man at a party. He was slightly above medium height, had dark hair combed to the side, and his face featured a square jaw, which gave him a strong masculine appearance. His front teeth protruded a little when he smiled, which made his grin seem bigger than it really was. His name was Melvin Sutherland.

When he saw me standing alone by the punch bowl, he made his way to me immediately. There was absolutely no hesitation, which I found a little disconcerting. I felt that he had an immediate advantage over me. He seemed so sure of himself, and was so confident that I would respond positively to his advances, that my first instinct was to push him away. Somehow, I couldn't. I felt powerless to resist his positive self-regard and the attention he was bestowing on me.

The way he looked at me with studied concentration, made him very appealing. I was also very curious about him. I couldn't help but wonder if his sincerity and confidence was real, or were these characteristics just the work of a master of deception.

Within a half hour we had abandoned the party and were sitting in a small diner close to the campus. The conversation we fell into for the next two hours consisted of a series of questions he asked about my interests, the classes I was taking, my family, and various other aspects related to my history. I was surprised by how curious he was about my background. I had never encountered a man who asked so many questions about me.

Most men wanted to talk about themselves and didn't really seem that curious about the girls they were dating. Mel seemed different. He asked me questions about my interests, and he invited me to inquire about his background. By the end of the evening I knew that he was a history major, that he played French horn in the college band, that he wanted to go to theological seminary after completing college, and that his ultimate goal was to become a minister in the Methodist Church. Texas was in the middle of the Bible Belt, as it still is today, and many young men in those times wanted to become a minister, more for the status it conveyed on them in the small rural towns where they grew up, than out of some deep religious conviction they held.

When he started talking about his aspirations, he seemed so enthusiastic and so confident. He exuded intelligence and maturity. He seemed to know something about everything. I'm almost certain now that my impressions of Mel were just the typical reaction of a freshman girl being taken in by a confident young man in his junior year, but at that time he impressed me as very worldly. I was clearly a naive eighteen year old girl with very little experience of the ways of a master manipulator. Looking back now, I know that Mel was very adept at sweeping women off their feet. I was far from his only conquest. There would be many more women after me who would fall into his trap.

Several months before we met, during the previous semester, his college band had gone on a two week trip to Europe. He told me all about the excursion and his experiences while abroad. I was totally mesmerized by each of the stories he told. Although he had only been out of the country for a grand total of fourteen days, the way he talked about Europe made him sound like such a world traveler.

As he expounded on his adventures in Germany, France and Switzerland, I started to feel a little uneasy and inferior. I was convinced that when he realized that my experience of the world was so limited he would loose interest in me quickly. I tried to sound smart and sophisticated, but most of the time I just couldn't think of anything to say, and wound up sitting there silently. I kept thinking to myself that surely he must see me as an absolutely stupid girl, but I couldn't seem to find a way of sounding more worldly.

When he took me back to my dorm, I stood awkwardly beside him. I couldn't make eye contact. I couldn't breath. Finally he put a hand on my arm. It seemed so hot I thought I would melt. Then, with a nonchalant air, he asked, "Would you like to go out again?"

I was absolutely dumbfounded. I couldn't believe that he was still attracted to me after seeing how uninteresting I was. I thought he would simply say that he had enjoyed the evening, and that maybe we would bump into each other again on campus. Surely, that would be the end of it, but he actually wanted to see me again.

I whispered a faint yes as I looked at the ground. He said "Great! That will be fun." And then he bent down and kissed me. I thought I would fall over, but the arm he put around me held me up. A second later he was bouncing down the sidewalk and into the dark. I stood there until I couldn't see him, and then I walked into the dorm. By the time I was ten steps inside the building I had to grab the wall to steady myself.

To this day I don't know how he was able to have such a powerful effect on me so quickly. I absolutely couldn't resist him. I felt like I was clay in his strong hands. When he talked, and he could talk like no other person I had ever known, I felt myself falling into a trance, carried along on the sound of his voice.

I felt like he was the exact opposite of me. I felt so insecure, so unsure about the future, really afraid of the world. I felt like there was always some catastrophe waiting around the corner, ready to pounce on me and knock me to the ground. By contrast, he was as confident as they came. Always upbeat, ready to take on any challenge, and so sure of his intelligence and talent.

Now, sixty years later, I can see what was really going on. He was a con artist, a brilliant and manipulative confidence man, able to sell you anything, and able to make you think that what he wanted to get from you was something you were more than eager to give him.

I now know that he had this way of spotting girls that were weak and unsure of themselves. My lack of confidence around him in those early days of our relationship was exactly what he was looking for. I was the perfect target, a girl who had been through hell in her teen years, a girl who was desperately trying to find stability, a girl desperately searching for a man to save her.

From that first night, to the dry, hot days of May, we were constantly together. Although he seemed genuinely interested in me, I kept thinking that he would discover that I wasn't half as fascinating as he had originally thought. When he asked me to marry him toward the end of the semester, during finals week, I was totally shocked. I kept asking myself, why would a man who was so confident, so experienced, so smart, who could sweep any girl he wanted off her feet, be interested in marrying mousy me. Of course, I said yes. I don't know how I could have turned him down, even if I had wanted to. By that point he held all the power and had complete control over me.

After the school year ended, I went back to El Paso and the home of the Isenhaths. It was the last place I wanted to go, but I had nowhere else that I could stay for the summer. Melvin went back to his home in Borger, Texas, in the northern part of the panhandle region. I wanted to tell the Isenhaths about Melvin and his marriage proposal, but I thought better of it. As it turned out, I was right. I knew I had to tell them at some point, but I thought that I should wait awhile. That proved to be very perceptive on my part. I fell back into my routine of locking myself in my room and reading for hours without pause.

I knew that I would have to tell them before I went back for my second year of college, and maybe I put it off too long. Finally, I realized I couldn't wait any longer. It was already the last weekend before I was scheduled to return, and I couldn't avoid the inevitable discussion. As dinner was wrapping up, and Edith was serving desert, I introduced the topic. They both dropped their forks in unison.

"What did you just say," Mr. Isenhath stated.

"I said that Melvin, this boy I met at McMurry, asked me to marry him, and I said yes."

"Wait a minute young lady," Mr. Isenhath replied, his voice growing more emphatic with each word. "We don't know anything about this young man. We didn't even know you had been dating anyone. How long has this relationship been going on, and what is this young man like. You can't just go off and marry someone like it was nothing of importance."

I explained that I had met him in February, and that we continued to date for the rest of the semester. During finals week he asked me to marry him, and I said yes. I further explained that he had written me several letters during the summer and wanted to set a wedding date for sometime this fall.

Mr. Isenhath slammed his fist on the table. "Listen to me young lady," he shouted. "This is totally unacceptable. You do not have permission to marry this man. Before you can get married I have to meet him. He should have met with me first and asked permission to ask you." He slammed the table again. "I don't like this young man already. He hasn't done things properly, and I don't like that."

I had guessed that this conversation would be difficult, but I hadn't anticipated quite this level of anger. I thought that they would be hesitant, and maybe even say that I should wait until I was older, or I had completed college, or something like that. I didn't think that Mr. Isenhath would burst into a rage. The more he thought about it the more his anger grew. He went from thinking about the lack of propriety in the man who had proposed to me to focusing his anger on how terrible I was. Soon, all his disgust with the situation was directed pointedly at me.

"I can't believe you would agree to this. Let me get this strait. You say that you have been seeing him for months now, and all the while we knew nothing of it. Why, in heaven's name, did you keep it from us. You are clearly hiding something. You aren't pregnant are you?"

I tried to answer, but he started in again before I could say a single word. "Have you been doing inappropriate things young lady? I can't believe this," he shouted. "We, in good faith, sent you to college to get a good education, a good religious education, and what do you do. You start running around, and doing I don't know what, with the first boy to come your way."

Soon his anger was also directed toward his poor wife, who sat there looking sheepish and afraid. "I warned you about this back when you were so sure that you wanted to adopt."

He was jabbing his finger to within inches of his poor wife's face. "It will be so wonderful to have a child you said. And I said then - I know you remember this conversation - I told you in no uncertain terms that orphaned children are ruined. They come from bad families and have no morals. They have been totally corrupted by their upbringing, and here is proof positive."

At one point I thought he might become violent. He was getting so worked up that his face turned a purplish red. In order to save the situation, and calm him down a little, I told him that I was sorry, and that I didn't realize I was doing anything wrong by accepting Mel's proposal. I assured him that I had done nothing that was improper and wouldn't think of doing anything like that. I then told him that I would tell Melvin that I couldn't marry him without their permission.

After several more biting comments directed at both of us, Mr. Isenhath finally settled down, but his anger was far from over. "Let me explain this to you in no uncertain terms young lady. If you marry this man, or have any further connections with him, we will refuse to pay another dime of your college education, and we will have nothing more to do with you. Do I make myself clear."

Chapter 10

Falling Down the Slippery Slope

I went back to college two days later, feeling devastated and depressed, and wondering what the future held for me. I didn't know what Mel would say or how he would react. When he arrived back at McMurry, I didn't say anything initially. I needed time to consider the situation, evaluate my options, and try to figure out what to do. He, of course, excited about our upcoming plans, was upbeat, and went on excessively about what it would be like to be married. It seemed like that was all he could talk about, and he made marriage sound like paradise.

As I listened to him go on about how we would soon be living in bliss, I wanted so much to just let myself go and fall into the fairy tale world he had created in his imagination, but all I could think about was my terrible dilemma. What should I do? How would Mel react if I said I couldn't marry him, at least for now? Or, if I went the other way and agreed to marry, how would the Isenhaths react? Would they follow through on their threat, and if they did, how would I be able to support myself?

About three weeks into the semester, I couldn't stand it anymore, and I told Mel about what had happened while I was home. I thought he would probably be mad at me and break off the relationship when

I explained to him that I had told the Isenhaths that I wouldn't marry him without their permission. I thought that he might reject me right there on the spot and tell me that he never wanted to see me again. Surprisingly, though, his reaction was very relaxed and almost casual.

"Emma, don't even worry about it," he said. "You don't even like being with them. Yes, I understand that they got you out of the orphanage, and they are paying for your college expenses. That doesn't mean you have to let them totally control your life. Clearly, Mr. Isenhath has a problem. The man has to be totally in control of every situation."

He continued on in his upbeat and confident tone. "Listen, do you still want to marry me?" he asked, as if he didn't already know the answer.

I whispered, "Yes, but I don't know if I can."

"Listen, there's absolutely no problem, no problem at all. I'll take care of you. I love you, and I will make sure that you are provided for. If you're my wife, I'm going to make sure that you are happy and have everything you need. I wouldn't be a good husband if I didn't do that."

His words sounded so reassuring, and his smile simply dissolved any objections I could muster in my head. I kept wondering how he, still in college, and by no means wealthy himself, could possibly provide for the two of us.

Over the next several weeks I kept asking him questions about where we would live and how we would afford it, how would he get a job and would he be able to stay in school. Notice that I didn't ask about my chances of staying in school. I figured out fairly quickly that I would have to drop out. Of course, in the 1950s, once a girl married that was the end of her college education. Social norms at that time made it clear that once you put that wedding ring on it was now time to be a wife and mother.

About the third week of October he invited me out to dinner at a nice restaurant in town. I immediately thought that something was up, and I was right. After we finished our meal, he announced, "I've worked out our plan. At the end of the semester, you and I are going to Borger. I've already taken care of all the arrangements. I had my mother and my older brother reserve a time for us at the Methodist church where my family attends. Our minister has agreed to perform the wedding ceremony. It's all set. All you have to do is pick out a nice wedding dress and show up."

I could feel my hands begin to tremble, and I quickly put them under the table so he wouldn't notice. I remember thinking to myself that something isn't right about this. I just had this strange premonition that marrying him was going to lead to some kind of disaster, but I couldn't identify what that disaster could possibly be. I went back and forth trying to understand my hesitation. I finally set aside these feeling as just nervousness, the kind of jitters that every girl must experience before they make the plunge into marriage.

I also wondered if a lot of my hesitation came from the fact that I had been sexually assaulted. I reasoned that going through that experience had made me worry about things other girls never considered. In the end I told myself that I had to go through with this and not let my past interfere with my future.

A few days later I wrote the Isenhaths and told them that, after much consideration, I had made the decision to marry Mel. I wrote that I hoped that they would forgive me for going ahead after I told them I wouldn't. I asked them to please understand that I loved Mel so much that I just couldn't live without him. I asked them to please accept my decision because I felt that I had to take this course, that ultimately it was the right thing to do. I ended the letter saying I hoped, even if they felt I was making the wrong decision, that they would find it in their hearts to accept my decision and come to the wedding in Borger.

About a week later I got a letter with a check enclosed. Mr. Isenhath stated emphatically that this would be the last check I would receive from them, and they wanted nothing more to do with me. I never spoke to them again.

At the end of the semester we loaded up Mel's old Chevy with several suitcases and other assorted items from our dorm rooms and headed north to Borger. I was very nervous about meeting his family, and could feel my agitation grow as we traveled up the long stretches of austere flatland so characteristic of the Texas Panhandle. Since it was mid-December, the countryside was desolate, grey, and barren. Every town we went through seemed almost empty, abandoned, and dusty. The only movement seemed to be the occasional stray tumbleweed. It almost seemed a gift from heaven when we passed a lonely farmhouse with a Christmas tree visible in the living room window.

As we approached Borger, the first thing we saw were billowing puffs of black smoke rising above the refineries. The town emerged almost overnight in the 1920s after oil was discovered nearby. A number of refineries now ringed the city. I asked Mel if his house was close to one of the refineries. I had visions of walking out the front door of his house and being choked by the black smoke. He assured me that his house was far from any of the refineries. "You can't even see them from where I live, but you can smell them," he said with a laugh.

I didn't find his comment funny, but I could see that he was more than pleased with himself. He went on about how, if you were downwind, you could smell Borger's refineries at least ten miles out of town. In addition to the smell, as we entered the outskirts of the town, you could actually see a light coating of black residue on all the buildings.

It was evident that he loved this polluted industrial wasteland he called his hometown. The main topic of conversation for much of the seven hour drive from Abilene had been discussions of his wonderful childhood in Borger. He had all kinds of stories to tell me about numerous friends and their youthful exploits. In each of these stories he was always the leader of the pack and the one who conjured up the various shenanigans they got into.

He also told a number of stories about his father. His dad, who had died when Mel was seventeen, was the greatest man alive, if you listened to Mel. He worshipped his father in a way that seemed extreme to the point of fantasy. At the time, I thought that maybe I just couldn't relate to his happy childhood given the fact that mine had been so different. I tried to imagine what it would have been like to have a wonderful father. My mind just wouldn't accept the concept.

When we arrived in his neighborhood, I began to absorb the reality of this drab town, and I quickly realized that it wasn't the fantasy version Mel presented. The street where he lived was a series of small and dirty white houses all lined up in a neat row along the street. They all had small front yards with dry yellowed grass, and many driveways featured old rusted cars and broken toys. These houses had been built by Phillips Petroleum Company in the 1930s to house the refinery workers. Everyone in the town worked for, or had a family member who worked for, Phillips, including Mel's older brother Edward, who was a loyal engineer for the company.

When we pulled into the driveway of Mel's house, my heart sank. Although painted white, like all the other houses on this street, the true color was closer to slate or dark grey. If the owner of houses in Borger didn't regularly clean, or repaint, the residue from the nearby refineries soon coated the entire exterior. Mel's house had clearly not been painted in quite some time. The front door, a dingy green color, was slightly ajar and was also in need of paint. The flower bed in front of the house was in disarray.

When we got out of the car, the family poured out of the house to greet us. All were in good spirits and happy to see us arrive. Mel introduced me to each person individually. First to make it to the car were his two sisters, Nora and Betty. Nora had large eyes and a wide mouth, with large teeth and gums that protruded when she smiled. The large front teeth angling forward seemed to be one of the prominent characteristics of the family and one of the things I had noticed about Mel when I first met him. Nora's hair was black, with a slight wave, and was cut short.

Betty was squat and a little overweight, with a wide face and dark hair pulled back in a bun. Next in line was Mel's mother, a small woman in her fifties, with dark hair streaked with grey. She had large thick glasses that made her eyes seem both huge and set back into her head. Then came Edward, Mel's older brother. He was large, well over six feet, heavy set, with a receding hairline, and a stubby face that constantly looked as though he needed a shave.

Everyone was very kind to me, and Mel's mother went on at length about how wonderful it was to meet me. She continued on for some time about how happy she was that Mel had found such a nice girl. I thought she was about to burst into tears, but Mel jumped in with a couple of jokes, and she was soon laughing along with the rest of the family.

Over the next several days I got to know the family well. I realized that Nora was rather slow, both mentally and physically. Whenever someone told a joke that she didn't comprehend, she would pout and grow increasingly angry until either Mel or Edward settled her down. She could also become moody if she felt like people were ignoring her. Her two brothers were the only people who could calm her down and bring back a cheerful mood. Edward had been successful in getting her a clerical job in the front office of one of the refineries. Apparently, she was largely incapable of doing the work she had been assigned, but Edward was close friends with her boss and had talked him into keeping her on the staff.

Betty was friendly, easygoing, and could be talkative when the conversation turned to Country and Western music. She had a strong Texas drawl to match her musical interests. She had married a Phillips worker right out of high school and was well on her way to adding several young children to the family. She eventually wound up conceiving five children. All would grow up and stay in and around Borger, working in various jobs around town.

On the day after our arrival, Betty revealed to me that she was pregnant, but explained that none of the men in the family knew yet. She hadn't even told her husband, Ollie, a quiet man, who seemed to be at work, or sleeping, most of the time. He rarely attended family gatherings. Apparently, he worked the graveyard shift at one of the refineries and was often asleep during the day.

Edward, Mel's brother, was ten years older than Mel and now clearly established as the head of the family. He was slow-moving, ponderous, and a little shy around women. I could tell he was a little afraid of me at first. Unlike most of the family, he was intelligent, hard working, and always measured in his decisions. With time, I grew to like him immensely and appreciate his calm demeanor, his measured response to family squabbles, and his reasoned leadership of the family. I believe strongly to this day that this family would have fallen apart without him.

Mel's mother was short, like her daughter Betty, but without Betty's soft roundness. Although numerous facial wrinkles indicated that she was clearly closing in on her sixties, she had managed to keep herself from becoming overweight like her daughter. She even exhibited a certain muscular strength in her shoulders. I attributed this to her early years and the hard work required of someone growing up on a dust bowl farm in Oklahoma.

From stories she told over the years, I knew her life had been very difficult on the farms that she and her husband John owned. Like so many farmers in those difficult times, they had lost their small stake in Oklahoma. Her husband then moved the family to a small wind-swept spread on the Texas panhandle, and within just a few years they lost that one as well.

That small farm on the Texas prairie was where Mel was born. When Mel was still just a baby, they had lived in a dugout shoveled out from the side of a small hill. One of the family tales Mel's mother told, and that I still remember so vividly to this day, was the story of her taking care of Mel when he was still just a newborn. She described in vivid detail a terrible dust storm that swept over the prairie. The sky actually turned light brown from all the dirt kicked up into the air.

She talked about how the dirt particles, blown around in twenty to thirty mile-per-hour gusts, actually stung the skin if you tried to walk outside. The poor baby was having trouble breathing from all the dust, so she took small pieces of wet cloth and wrapped them around the face of the baby to keep the dust away. I had remembered those dust storms myself when I lived on the farm near Hamlin. Those were certainly difficult times during the Dust Bowl era.

John, the now deceased father of Mel, was, in the eyes of the family, first cousin to God himself. If you listened to family members long enough, you would have been convinced that he walked on water, performed multiple miracles, and was the wisest person on the planet. He was especially known for his witty aphorisms, and home-grown folkloric sayings that the family liked to quote on a regular basis. The one that I heard from almost every member of the family at one time or another gives a good idea of the experiences this family endured during those early years on the two farms. John often stated, while his family listened with rapt attention, "The West offers a thousand opportunities to get rich, so long as you were able to survive dust storms, blizzards, droughts, crop failures, and bill collectors."

After the loss of the the second farm, the family was saved from complete destitution when John found work in one of the Philips Petroleum Company's refineries. It was during the bleak years of the Depression when job openings were practically nonexistent, but John succeeded in acquiring a position in one of the refineries by getting up at 4 a.m. every morning, walking to the gate of the refinery and asking if there was work he could do. Every morning he was told that there was nothing.

One winter morning, with temperatures hovering just above freezing, one of the other workers failed to show up for work. Since the refinery manager had seen him standing at the gate so many times, he offered to let him take the tardy worker's place. It was his foot in the door, and for the next nine years, through the difficult times of the depression, and during World War II, the family prospered with the good income John brought in from his refinery job.

But tragedy struck the family when John, then just 50 years old, was killed in a refinery accident in 1945. Apparently, a steel beam being moved by a crane, hit him in the back of the head and knocked him off a construction scaffold some thirty feet off the ground. Refinery accidents like this weren't that uncommon back in those days, but the community accepted them as the price of doing business. No one was willing to fight the company over serious safety issues at most of the refineries since almost everyone worked there and relied on the jobs provided by the company.

After John's death, he became an almost mythic hero in the family's eyes. Edward talked about him as a soft-spoken man, who was wise, solid, and a great leader. Mel's two sisters talked in awe about how kind and gentle he was. Mel, who was only seventeen at the time of his death, talked about him as a wonderful father who taught him so much about life.

Mel's mother fell apart after the accident and never recovered completely from the loss of her beloved husband. As strong as she had been in her early years as a farmer's wife, since the accident she had become almost an invalid. Edward, who was already in his late twenties when the accident took place, and working in a good job as an engineer for Philips, took care of her and provided her with everything she needed. Although he certainly had the income to strike out on his own, he continued to live at home and never dated. Mel even tried to fix him up with a date on several occasions, but he always turned down the offers. "What woman would want me," he would always say, and that would be the end of the discussion.

As I heard all these tales of life on the farms, the move to Borger, life during World War II, and the loss of their hero father, I kept telling myself that I should be thrilled to be accepted into such a family. Who was I to complain. My family made Mel's relatives seem absolutely wonderful by comparison. Yet, I couldn't keep from thinking that there was something dreadful and dreary about this group of people. Although Mel's brother Edward seemed genuinely solid and good-natured, the women, Mel's mother and two sisters, seemed somewhat strange to me in a way that I couldn't quite identify. I kept thinking that someone was going to rush into the room, pull back the curtain, and reveal our true location in a lunatic asylum.

Now Mel, the youngest sibling, and clearly doted on by his mother and sisters, began to seem strange himself. He was so much more lively, more intellectual, more interesting overall than the rest of his family. At the same time, the hard luck that he and the family had experienced, and his total worship of his father, made me feel that there was something that was slightly unstable in his personality. Yet, at that point, I couldn't identify just what was wrong with him.

Looking back now, I think his intellectual interests covered up certain queer personality traits that surfaced ever so slightly when he was at home. At college, Mel and I talked for hours about what we were studying, about the books we were reading for our classes, about the latest movies we had seen. Now, I was seeing a different side of Mel.

85

The women in the family spoiled him and treated him as a child. He was always the center of attention. Anything he wanted they were only too happy to obtain for him. And yet, he could be cruel, especially to his sister Nora, when she failed to understand something said at the dinner table. When he was alone with me, he would often make cutting remarks about how dumb everyone in his family was. He loved the attention they gave him, at the same time that he seemed to hate them as stupid and slow.

As the wedding day approached, I tried to banish all these thoughts from my head and dream about how wonderful life would be once I was married to Mel. I still worried about how we were going to put food on the table, and how we were going to pay for a place to live while he finished his last semester, but Mel kept assuring me that there was nothing to worry about.

On the night before our wedding day, I finally found out how Mel had been so sure that everything would be fine. Mel had convinced Edward to "loan" him enough money to pay our expenses for at least six months, but I didn't find that out from Mel. While everyone else was in the kitchen, Edward and I had taken our drinks into the living room. He plopped down in his favorite chair, I found a place on the sofa opposite his chair.

After a few minutes of friendly conversation, he leaned toward me and whispered, "I hope the money I loaned Mel will be enough to get the two of you off to a good start. I know how hard it is getting started and establishing a nice home. If you find yourself running short for any reason just give me a call."

I was startled. "Wait a minute," I said. "You loaned money to Mel? I didn't know."

"Oh" he said, and pulled back in his seat with a confused expression. "I," he hesitated, and then cleared his throat. "I thought you knew, I thought Mel had told you of our arrangement."

"No," I replied, "I really had no idea. Mel never said a word to me about any kind of loan." There was a long silence while we both tried to process this new information. Edward was clearly uncomfortable and shifted uneasily in his chair.

He finally gained his composure. "Well, I guess he wanted to surprise you." He cleared his throat again. "Maybe he thought that telling you later would be a good surprise to announce after the wedding." He looked up to check my response, worried about how I would react.

I smiled. "Yes, I'm sure he didn't want me to worry," I said in order to make him feel at ease. I didn't want Edward to feel bad about telling me something that Mel had wanted to keep secret, so I tried to reply in a very casual, light-hearted manner. "Yes, I'm sure that Mel planned to tell me after the wedding. That's just like him," I laughed. "He always likes to surprise me."

As I sat there waiting for the others to finish preparations for dinner, I felt very uneasy. Edward's idea seemed like a plausible explanation, but I couldn't help but suspect that Mel didn't want me to know that he had to borrow money from his brother. He had made such a production out of telling me repeatedly that he was going to be a good provider, that he would take care of me. I immediately felt that Mel hadn't been honest with me, and I began to wonder what else he had chosen not to tell me.

All these worries, these constant feelings that some things weren't as they should be, and these little hints that Mel wasn't exactly the person that I thought he was, simply wouldn't go away. They kept surfacing in my mind and in my dreams each night. Of course, I did what a lot of young, naive women do in this situation. I just kept repeating to myself that it was pre-wedding jitters, and that I needed to calm down. I was simply worrying about little things that really didn't matter. I kept telling myself that everything would be fine.

Finally, our wedding day arrived. Believe me, it was nothing special. Of course, I woke up early and couldn't go back to sleep. Finally, after staying in bed until I heard others stirring, I got up and went down to the kitchen. There, I had a light breakfast with Mel's mother, who was polite, but wasn't as animated and talkative as usual. I think she was confronting the inevitable emotions that most mothers face when one of her sons is about to get married. After managing to swallow a few bites, I went back to my bedroom, and with the assistance of Betty, I put on my wedding dress. When I looked in the mirror I almost didn't recognize myself. I felt like I was looking at some make-believe doll that wasn't really real.

We had a small ceremony in the Methodist Church with the family and a few of Mel's friends in attendance. Of course, no one from my family was there. After the ceremony, we all went to a local restaurant for the reception. Toward the end of the dinner, while Mel talked with a few of his friends, I remember looking out over the small assembled group and feeling very sad. Was this the beautiful moment that every girl dreamed of having on her wedding day?

In my fantasies I had imagined that weddings were supposed to be momentous occasions of sheer bliss, the best day in a woman's life. But everything, Mel, Mel's family, this town, these people, all seemed so common, so strange. I remember chastising myself for not appreciating what I had. Many girls had nothing I told myself. But I still couldn't shake the feeling that I wanted something deeper, something full and positive, something that was somehow rich and beautiful. I just didn't know what it was or how to find it.

That evening we left for Amarillo, about an hour's drive south of Borger. Mel had reserved a room in a downtown hotel. By the time we got there it was already dark, and the town was largely deserted. A few Christmas lights in storefront windows provided the only color and cheer in the scene. I wanted to cry, but the tears wouldn't come.

Chapter 11

The Early Years of Marriage

At this point it was lunch time, and Emma and I decided that it was time to take a break. I offered to take her to a nice restaurant just around the corner, and I suggested that "while we're at it we can stop in a few galleries and see what the competition is up to." She liked that idea immensely, and we headed out within the next few minutes.

After a light lunch, where we talked about the art market and the extraordinary prices for some of the art being sold at the art fairs around the world, we walked around the neighborhood. As we made our way around, we stopped in several of the numerous galleries that dot the neighborhood close to my gallery. It was great fun. Emma was a delightful person to spend time cruising the galleries around Chelsea.

Of course, most of the art we saw was dreadfully awful, as I warned her it would be, but we had a great time making fun of a lot of what we saw. She could drop a funny line about a bad painting faster than anyone I knew. She was also very perceptive when we saw something we thought was good. Emma had a keen eye, and she could identify exactly the specific features that made a painting successful. She also could put together an analysis in a few sentences that would have impressed even an art critic.

It was also very interesting to hear her compare the Chelsea galleries of today, with all their slickness and overblown style, to what she remembered of the Soho art scene back in the 70s. She kept mentioning how everything was so much dirtier and rundown then. "Most of the galleries back in that day were usually down some back alley, and were quite often located in an old rundown building with graffiti all over the outside."

She talked about the gallery where she had exhibited. "I can still remember walking into that gallery when I first arrived in New York and seeing a bunch of boxes in the corner," she laughed. "Boxes of merchandise were left from the factory that had occupied the space prior to the gallery taking over the location."

I told her that if she had been in New York just a few years later I very well could have been one of the receptionists who greeted her when she walked into the gallery where I worked. "I lived and worked in Soho for many years. In fact, since you lived there as well, we could have been neighbors."

After we finished our gallery visits it was the middle of the afternoon, and we made our way back to my apartment. Once we were again settled comfortably in my living room, with a cup of tea in hand, I urged her to continue her story. I started the discussion by asking her about her early years as a wife. She began with a question that I'm sure many young women have asked themselves many times.

Why did I marry him when I was still so unsure of my own feelings? I've asked myself that question a thousand times over the years, and to this day I'm not really sure. Maybe, I was just young and naive. Maybe, it was simply the times. You have to keep in mind what it was like after the war. All my girlfriends were getting married or planning to marry soon. Women in those days were expected to get married as soon as possible.

That was considered the only course for a young woman. We were told time and time again that marriage was the only way to insure long-term happiness. You didn't want to wind up an old maid. That was a nightmare scenario. If you weren't married by the age of 24 or 25, you were dangerously close to old maid status.

I think I realized that I was different from the other girls I knew. I didn't spend every minute of the day dreaming of domestic bliss. Somehow the vision of cooking perfect dinners every evening for a darling husband didn't appeal to me at all. But I worried why I was the only girl I knew who didn't have that dream.

I knew I was somewhat adrift, but I think I saw Mel as someone who might bring stability to my life. His confidence, as well as his focus on being successful, seemed like what I needed to balance my ambivalent relationship to the world around me. I knew that I was an outsider, already extremely critical of life in rural Texas. Yet, at this stage, I simply didn't know what to do with myself, or where I could go to change my situation. I kept thinking that maybe once I had a successful husband, and a nice house with a white picket fence, and maybe two or three adorable children, I would finally be happy and content.

Of course, this marriage was doomed before it ever began. The first several months were awful. The horror began on our wedding night in that bleak hotel room in Amarillo. As soon as we were in bed, Mel just climbed on top of me and started pushing. I tried to adjust to his clumsy moves and just relax, but he forced himself on me so quickly that all I could feel was grinding discomfort.

We returned to Abilene for Mel's last semester the next day. I threw myself into fixing up our small rented house, and ended up most afternoons sitting alone in the back yard with a drink in my hand. I didn't blame my unhappiness on Mel. I thought it was all my fault. I saw myself as a misfit unable to adjust to a normal married life. I kept telling myself that I should be happy. I had a husband, I had a nice house. What was wrong with me that made me so unsatisfied with what many others dream of having?

Through a mixture of domestic routine, meeting with my girlfriends whenever I could, and growing amounts of alcohol, I settled into a state of dull, dreary unhappiness. Sex with Mel continued to be uncomfortable. The whole process seemed so crude. He was very aggressive, and when he rolled on top of me I felt like I was an object he was trying to attack. But I kept thinking that it must be my fault.

Since I had been molested, I thought that I was unable to enjoy sex. I sometime felt that I was damaged beyond repair.

At that point in my life, I didn't have the slightest idea what a sexual climax felt like. Of course, that was something that no one talked about then. It would never have occurred to me to ask one of my girlfriends what sex was like for them. Knowing what I know now, probably most of them weren't having the greatest sex either.

On evenings when we ate at home, I would try to fix a nice dinner for Mel. I would make sure that the table was set perfectly, that all the dishes were hot and ready to serve once he came in from school, and I would always light a candle for the table. I'm fairly certain that he rarely noticed my effort. He certainly never said anything to indicate that he took note of all my planning. I think he just took the whole process for granted. His mother had done these things for him, so why shouldn't his wife do the same thing.

I was soon to discover that he saw the world in very conventional terms. According to his way of thinking, men were supposed to leave in the morning, put in a hard day at the office, and then come home to a wife who's job was to prepare an excellent dinner. As long as the man did what he was supposed to do, and the woman did what she was supposed to do, the world kept clicking along smoothly and everyone was fantastically happy.

After a few months, I noticed that many of my girlfriends were getting pregnant. These were the baby boom years, and it seemed like every day another one of my friends announced that she was expecting. They always seemed so happy as they discussed the good news. In short order I began to think that maybe that was the key to my happiness.

I started trying to get pregnant, but it just didn't happen. I thought that maybe nature wasn't taking it's course because I disliked having sex with Mel, that somehow my body was resisting the whole process. I tried to relax, and I tried to think positive thoughts, but nothing happened. I was soon berating myself as a terrible person. My inability to get pregnant must be an indication that I deserved my lot.

Then, just when I was about to give up hope, I was pregnant. On a steamy Texas day in May, seventeen months after we married, I gave birth to a beautiful baby boy. We named him Gary, and I think that for the first time since I was a child I was truly happy. I just loved this little person who came so abruptly into my life. Each day seemed like a completely new adventure, and with great curiosity I studied his phenomenal growth and daily changes with utter fascination.

Gary was a quiet, good natured baby, and he was very easy to take care of as a child. But with any baby there are times a new mother needs support. I kept asking Mel to help out when he came home. By that time of day I was exhausted, but my pleas were useless. At 6 or 6:30 p.m. Mel would saunter into the house, pick up the newspaper, and plop down into his easy chair asking what was for dinner. There were times I felt like serving him dinner by throwing it at him, but I stayed patient. I was bound and determined to be a good mother and a good wife. I kept trying to convince myself that if I stayed devoted to my domestic responsibilities I would find fulfillment and be happy.

Needless to say, the bliss I dreamed of never came. The afternoon cocktail soon became two or three cocktails before Mel arrived on the scene. Many of my evenings with Mel became a hazy blur. I must say that I never became drunk to the point that it was noticeable. In fact, I was very good at acting perfectly normal while I was intoxicated. I'm almost certain that Mel never became alarmed at how much I was drinking. Of course, he wasn't the most observant individual. He never seemed to notice much of anything anyway. While he read the newspaper, or listened to the radio (we still didn't have one of those new televisions), I could have stood on my head, and he wouldn't have noticed a thing.

Mel, who seemed to grow into the traditional husband and father role more and more with each passing day, liked having a child. A bouncing baby boy and a nice wife were indications of his success as far as he was concerned. In public, he was always assuming the part of the wonderful husband and father. What a wonderful man our friends and neighbors must have thought he was. I began to wonder how things could look so perfect from the outside and be so wrong behind closed doors.

Most women were just like me, very good at presenting the perfect picture of domestic bliss. Often, just a small crack in their facade would let me see underneath the surface of their smiling faces. One day a neighbor asked if I had seen her husband with another woman. "It was probably nothing," she said with a forced smile, "I was just curious," she commented, like it was just a casual question.

On another occasion, a college girlfriend came to visit and asked if she could stay a couple of days. Her husband wasn't feeling well she said, and she just thought it would be a good idea to let him have some time alone. A black eye covered up with a lot of makeup, and several bruises on her arm, indicated that something else was going on.

Of course, it wasn't just the women who began to reveal cracks in our suburban bliss. At a summer backyard party, a man who lived just three doors down from us made a pass at me while my husband was inside getting a drink. I asked him what his wife would think, and he replied that she didn't need to know. I thought to myself - how much do all of us not know about what the rest of us are doing and thinking.

I started to ask myself why America was turning into this false paradise. Materially, we were much richer than people from other countries, and we were so much better off than our parents, who had been forced to endure the Great Depression. We had nice jobs, nice houses, nice cars, and nice children. We were getting college degrees at a much higher rate than the previous generation. With all this to be thankful for, why were so many of us so unhappy?

These observations make me think of a comment I once read by the novelist Walker Percy. He said, "Why does man feel so bad in the very age when, more than any other age, he has succeeded in satisfying his needs and making over the world for his own use?"

After Mel graduated, he got a job as a part-time minister and a teacher. His grand plan was to become a Methodist minister. In order to do that, he needed to attend a seminary program. He wanted to go to the Perkins School of Theology in Dallas, but being short of money he asked the regional bishop of the Methodist Church to give him what they then called a pre-seminary appointment.

Since there weren't enough ministers for every church, many of the small congregations in remote rural locations weren't able to attract a fully qualified seminary graduate to their community. The church rectified the situation by appointing young men, recently out of college, to serve as the minister for these rural congregations while they attended seminary, or before they began the program.

Since money was very tight, Mel asked to delay his start at Perkins for one year. That allowed him to accept, along with his church appointment, a teaching position in the town's rural high school. With two incomes, we hoped to be able to save a little money so that Mel could go back to school in a year or two.

So we moved to a little spot in the road called Lueders, Texas. This tiny village, with maybe fifteen streets, most unpaved, had a population of, at best, five hundred people. Even with so small a population, the local citizens were very proud of the fact that the town had eight churches. Since we were in the middle of the Bible Belt, it seemed as if there was a church on every other block. I often wondered if the ranchers, who laid out the settlement's first streets in the last decade of the nineteenth century, planned the town with the idea that there would be so many churches.

The church he was assigned was the First Methodist Church of Lueders. It was a small congregation, and when I mean small I mean that the entire membership, including children, was between fifty and sixty souls at any one time. Given the fact that most of the young people were leaving town and moving to Dallas or Houston as soon as they finished high school, the congregation tended to be a lot of old farmers and their wives.

I have to say that I was very surprised when Mel gave his first sermon. I had never heard him speak in public before. He was actually very good at it, and he seemed to have his congregation following his every word. He started out reading a short passage from the Bible, then he began to elaborate on the passage, picking out bits of special interest. Then he turned his attention to the message he wanted to convey and came right to the point. As he neared the climax of his sermon his voice grew louder and more intense, and I could see a few heads in the pews bobbing up and down in agreement. I was really impressed with the whole delivery and wondered how he learned to do this.

I was also somewhat taken aback by a number of his statements during the sermon. I had never heard Mel talk so vehemently about the literal truth of the Bible, being led astray by the devil, and the terrible price to pay for sinning. The few times we had discussed religion Mel had argued that the Bible wasn't literally true, as so many people believed. He argued that it was just an inspirational text and must be understood in the context of the times it was written. He clearly looked down on these rural folk, stating that their religious convictions were the "simple beliefs of simple people."

But here he was giving a fire and brimstone sermon and talking about the literal truth of the Bible. Although I knew he didn't believe many of the things he was saying from the pulpit, he certainly sounded convincing. In fact, he was so convincing I remember wondering if I had misunderstood some of things he had said when we talked about theology.

Later, when I asked him about the seeming disparities between what he had said to me and what he said in the sermon, he gave me a look like an adult trying to explain something complicated to a young child. "You must understand that you have to reach people on their own level." He paused to see if I was understanding and then explained further. "You see, I have to make these simple farming folk feel that I am one of them, that I believe what they do."

At the time, what he said seemed convincing, and I accepted it. But I remember feeling somewhat uneasy. It just seemed like he was telling them what they wanted to hear. He wasn't trying to assert what he really believed, and I began to wonder if this was what one had to do to be a successful minister. I also wondered how one could continue to assert ideas, week after week, sermon after sermon, that were so inconsistent with what one really believed.

Mel also proved very successful as a teacher. Since Lueders High School was a very small school, the teachers were expected to teach whatever subjects were required by the school. Mel wound up teaching history, since that had been his major in college, music, since he had played in the college band, and he was selected to be the football coach, since he was the only teacher willing to do it.

He told me that he had never played football in school, but before long he was telling all the boys on the team about his exploits as a football player in high school. I worried about what the consequences would be if someone found out that he hadn't really played football in his school years. Yet, as I thought it through, I reasoned that maybe it was necessary to say these things, to fudge the truth a little, in order to convince his team that he could capably coach them.

And coach them he did. The school had suffered through a dismal two win and eight loss season the year before. He turned that around and led the team to a seven win and three loss season. The music program also took off. He somehow convinced a bunch of kids to sign up for the band program, and soon many of the students felt that if you weren't on the football team you had to be in the band. By the middle of the school year people were telling me that he was the most popular teacher in the school.

After what seemed to be such a successful year, just a few weeks before the end of the school year, and just a couple of weeks before I was due to deliver our first child, he came home one day and announced that we were moving. He explained that there was a problem at school, and that they weren't renewing his contract for next year. He also stated that the elders at the church had asked him to leave.

I was stunned. At first he wouldn't tell me what had gone wrong. Eventually, he explained that there had been an "incident," with one of his students. The way he put it seemed very strange to me. According to his explanation, one of the girls in his music class had a crush on him. He kept resisting her, but in a moment of weakness he had given in and had made love to her. I remember clearly. He said they had "made love," not "had sex."

I remember that I was sitting at our kitchen table in our small rented house, a glass of iced tea in front of me, beads of water streaming down the sides of the glass. I couldn't move. I just kept staring at the glass of tea that I had been about to drink, but now couldn't even consider sipping. The room around me began to turn black, and soon all I could see was the glass of tea. Then, all of a sudden, my arm jerked, and the glass of tea flew across the table and on to the floor. Mel, standing at the kitchen sink, looked stunned. I was stunned. I had no idea that I was going to do that. But it brought my mind back to a state of consciousness where I could at least think about what was happening, or what had happened.

For a minute or two Mel just stood there looking back and forth at me and at the broken tea glass strewn across the floor. He stayed in place, afraid to move closer to me, and in that interval I began to think about what this meant. Here I was, married to this man for less than a year-and-a-half, and he already had been unfaithful. On top of all that, in less than two weeks I was to give birth to his child. What do I do now?

I wondered what the proper response was for a young wife in this situation. Do I scream and shout? Do I slap him? Do I cry? Do I throw dishes? Or, do I just sit there and try to act rational? Am I supposed to be the good wife and forgive him for having a moment of weakness? I didn't do any of those things. I just stood up, walked out of the room, closed the door of our bedroom, and went to bed. I stayed there until well into the next morning.

When I finally came out of the bedroom, I looked around the house to make sure Mel wasn't there. At that point I thought about just packing a bag and leaving, but then I asked myself where I could possibly go. I had nowhere to run, no one to stay with, no one who would take me in. I was alone, stuck with this man who had just betrayed me. How could I possibly make it on my own with a baby on the way? For the first time in my life I thought about killing myself, but I just couldn't do that to the baby inside of me. I had to stay alive for my baby.

Mel came back in the early evening. I was sitting in the living room waiting for him. I could hear the back door open slowly, carefully. I could tell, just from the way he walked through the kitchen, that he was nervous about how I would react when he came into the room. I was sitting in the dark. It was still the early evening, so there was just enough light to be able to see, but when he walked into the room I could tell that the lack of light bothered him. After looking nervously around the room he sat down opposite me. For a few minutes we just sat there, not saying anything, or doing anything.

I finally began the conversation. "I want you to tell me everything. I don't want to have to guess what has been going on. I don't want my imagination to run wild wondering what you did and who you did it with. Just tell me the truth. What did you do?"

"Emma, I'm sorry," he began. "I didn't want to put you through this. I didn't want you to have to know."

"Stop, just stop!" I put my hand up as if I was blocking his voice from coming near me. "I don't want to hear you apologizing, I don't want to hear you tell me how you didn't want to hurt me. If you cared about that you wouldn't have done what you did in the first place. Just tell me what you did. Tell me everything you did. Don't try to make me feel better. You can't do that. Just tell me what you did."

He took in a deep breath, shifted in his chair, then cleared his throat. "This girl, a senior this year, plays in the band and is in my music class. I guess she had a crush on me. She kept asking for help after school. She plays the clarinet. She wanted me to give her private lessons to help her improve, so I started working with her after school."

He cleared his throat once again. He was clearly nervous. "One day, after we had been working on a difficult passage in the piece she was trying to learn, we stopped and took a break. She started talking about how hard school was for her. She was worried about what to do after high school. She didn't know if she wanted to go to college. She said that she would really like to major in music, but she didn't know if she could do it. I felt sorry for her. Then the next thing I knew I was kissing her."

He paused and looked up at me to see how I was reacting. I just sat there and stared at him, not moving a muscle.

He continued. "And then the next thing I know clothes were coming off and ..." he paused and then whispered, "we made love."

I jerked. "Why do you keep saying that? Why do you keep saying that you 'made love?' You had sex with her, you stuck your fucking cock in her cunt. That's what you did. Say that!" I shouted.

99

Obviously flustered he stuttered, "Ok." He paused again. "I had ..." he could hardly get the words out, "I had sex with her." He cleared his throat and nervously ran his hand through his hair, trying to regain his composure. "But it only happened once. I swear, it only happened once."

"Why?" I asked. "If she had a crush on you, why didn't she come back for more? She must have been so happy to finally win the jack pot and 'make love' - as you say. Are you telling me the truth? You only did it once?"

"I swear," he said emphatically, "we only did it once. After that one time, she stopped asking to work with me after school. I think we both realized that it wasn't a good idea."

"Or maybe she really didn't want to have sex with you," I said, my voice increasing in intensity. "Just because a teenage girl has a crush on her teacher doesn't mean she really wants to get down on the floor and fuck. At that age, a crush is just a fantasy. It isn't at all about the dirty, sloppy reality of adult sex. Don't you know that?"

"You're right, you're absolutely right. I just lost my head."

"You lost more than your head."

He sat back not knowing what to say.

When I think back to this evening, I don't know how I was able to say these things to him so directly. I guess it was just raw anger. I had never talked to him like this before. I had always been so caught in his spell.

After a few minutes of sitting silently I began again. "So how did the School Superintendent find out?"

"Well," he began, "apparently she told her father. I don't know why she did that, but she did. Her father went to the Superintendent and told him that he wanted me fired, but he didn't want to make the reason public. He was worried about what this would do to his daughter's reputation if it got out. He said that if I wasn't fired he would take legal action, but he didn't want to do that. Consequently, I was called in and told that I had the option to quit on my own and agree to say nothing about the girl, or, if I didn't agree to those terms, they would fire me, and I would never be able to teach again. So I agreed."

"But what happened at the church?" I asked.

"Apparently, her father went to one of the church elders and told him the same thing. They took the same approach. They asked me to resign."

"What do we do now?" I asked. "Did you ever think about the fact that I'm pregnant? When you were fucking her, did that ever cross your mind?"

"Please, don't worry," he replied. "I found a job in Fritch, just fifteen miles from Borger. The bishop agreed to give me another chance. He said that the church in Fritch needed a new minister, and he felt that I would be perfect for the job. I was also able to find a new teaching job. When the high school superintendent and principle heard that I was moving to town and would be available to teach, they were delighted. I'm going to be their new music teacher this next school year.

That's not all. My brother said he would help us find a place to live. We're going to be fine," he replied in his usual convivial manner, a tone that made me want to slap him.

I finally reconciled myself to the situation and accepted the fact that I had nowhere else to go. I had no conceivable way to support a baby. About a week after this awful conversation, I was at the supermarket loading my bags of groceries in the back seat of the car when, all of a sudden, I felt someone directly behind me. I raised up, and a middle-aged women was standing so close to me that I could hardly move. I felt like I might actually fall into the car if she stepped any closer.

"I just want you to know that your husband raped my daughter," she spit out in a sharp voice that hissed through the air. "How can you live with such a man?" She then turned her back and walked quickly away. I got into the car as fast as I could and locked the doors. I just sat there crying. The next day I gave birth to our first son.

Chapter 12

Life in Fritch, Texas

With the new baby just a month old, we loaded a rented truck with our things and set out for our new home in Fritch, Texas. The house that Mel's brother found for us was a spacious, up-to-date house on an unpaved street a couple of blocks off the main road. The house was just a few years old, and I had to complement Mel's brother on the choice. Edward bought the house with cash that he had saved and told Mel that he could start making payments whenever we got back on our feet and had a steady income. I thought to myself that we were so lucky to have Mel's brother. I don't know how we would have made it at that time without his help.

Within a week of our arrival, Mel assumed his duties at the First Methodist Church in Fritch, and as expected, his first sermon was a fire-and-brimstone tirade very similar to the one he gave on that first Sunday in Lueders. It was crystal clear to me by then that the ideas expressed with such seeming conviction in his sermons had absolutely nothing to do with what he really believed. He was just telling people what they wanted to hear. He also took over the church music program and assumed the duties as choir director.

For the first few weeks I was inundated with people telling me how talented he was, how great a minister he was, and how lucky I was to be married to such a wonderful person. I just smiled and thanked them for their kind comments.

The fact that we were a young, attractive couple, with a brand new adorable baby, just made him seem all the more perfect. We were the town's new perfect couple. Since he had such a wonderful wife and such a perfect little baby, he must be everything that he seemed to be in the pulpit and the classroom. When people bumped into us on the street, or in the grocery store, you could just see them begin to glow, like they were receiving a gift from heaven.

People, especially women, would practically swoon in his presence, and I marveled at how utterly wrong the public's perception was from the private reality. After awhile, these encounters with town folk became very disturbing for me, and I reached a point that I hated going out in public with him. Of course, it was unavoidable. I had to make my weekly appearance at church, I had to attend high school football games with him, and show up for other events where he was the center of attention.

In September Mel started teaching music at Fritch High School, and as before, he was soon one of the most popular teachers at the school. Everyone was just so enamored with him. How could I blame them. I too had found his personality magnetic when we were first dating. Even after the affair with the girl, I sometimes found his charm irresistible. But around this time, I also began to feel that his ability to charm people was somehow sinister. With every passing day, I became more and more convinced that he didn't really believe many of the things he said, and that he used his charm on people in order to take advantage of them.

Of course, in those days, I had little time to contemplate all these questions. I was busy night and day taking care of a brand new baby. He was adorable, and I loved him dearly. But it was sometimes hard to devote the energy I needed to this active little person. I couldn't get the thought of Mel having sex with that girl out of my mind, and I wondered if it might happen again. At football games it seemed like half the girls in the band wanted attention from Mel.

Then, I started to worry that it might be my fault. Maybe the reason he had sex with that girl while I was pregnant was because I was fat and ugly. I had heard that men sometimes strayed when a wife was pregnant, or taking care of a new child, and, of course, our sex life was strained, to say the least. There were times I just couldn't stand the thought of having sex, so I resisted his advances as much as I could.

On a couple of occasions, Mel said that the reason I didn't want to have sex was because of what had happened to me when I was a teenager. He said that I needed to forget that and not think of sex in a negative way. He insisted that he could help me, and show me how to have enjoyable sex.

I felt like he got the whole situation wrong. Yes, the trauma of what happened with my uncle had certainly left a scar, but I really wanted to have good sex with Mel. I wanted to feel loved by him. Yet, I never felt totally comfortable with him in bed. His wonderful charm at church and at school just didn't translate to good experiences in the bedroom, at least for me. When we had sex, he seemed so aggressive and focused on his own pleasure. I often felt that I was just an object to be taken and devoured.

These issues in the bedroom, as well as his infidelity with the high school girl, made me vow to try to be the best wife I could be, to make him happy, to give him whatever he wanted, to never say no to him. Maybe, if I was really devoted to Mel, he would be so happy at home that he would never want to think about doing anything with another woman. For the next several months, every time he approached me wanting sex, I said yes. Quite often it was all I could do just to endure the experience. There were times that our lovemaking actually hurt, but I just closed my eyes, clenched my teeth, and got through it.

Then, when little Gary was about six months old, it happened again. It was a Thursday evening, choir practice night. Mel was at the church, I was home taking care of the baby. On this particular evening I was bored sitting around the house. I had been trapped in the house all day, and it was a beautiful evening. I decided to walk to the church, meet Mel after he finished choir practice, and then I could ride back home with him.

As I approached the church, with the baby on my arm, I noticed that a man and woman were sitting in a car in the church parking lot. As I got closer, I realized that it was Mel and a woman from the choir. I stopped dead on the sidewalk and watched. They were facing the other direction, so they couldn't see me. I didn't have to wait long. They were soon kissing. I felt my knees buckle, and I almost dropped the baby. I just sat down right there on the ground and tried to pull air back into my lungs. It was getting dark, and I just sat there and watched them. After a minute or two I simply couldn't stand it anymore. I got up and walked home.

After I got home, I put the baby to bed and then sat down at the kitchen table, waiting for him to come home. I went over a thousand scenarios in my mind. Do I confront him directly? Do I ask him what he was doing and wait for him to lie to me? Do I refuse to talk to him? I couldn't think clearly. My mind was in such a muddle that nothing seemed clear.

All my thinking had been to no purpose anyway. As soon as he walked in the door, my emotions took over, and I immediately began to cry. He stood there not knowing how to react. Finally, through my sobs I choked out, "I saw you with that woman. I saw you kiss her. I saw you. How could you?"

This time around he was a lot more prepared than the first time we had had this conversation. He immediately sat down beside me and put his hand on my arm.

"Oh Emma," he began, "you didn't see what you thought you saw. I know what you're thinking, and after what happened before, I can understand why you would think such a thing. But that's not what was going on. That was Betty DeVries. You know her from church. She's going through a bad time. She's having trouble in her marriage, and she turned to me for advice. She respects me, and she felt that maybe I could help her. I was just talking to her and trying to console her."

"You don't kiss someone you're consoling," I yelled.

"I wasn't kissing her, I really wasn't," he said in a calm, even tone. I felt like he was talking to me like you would talk to a child you're trying to settle down after a temper tantrum. "I was just giving her a hug because she was so upset. It may have looked like I was kissing her, but I wasn't."

At first I didn't know how to respond to what he was saying. He had thrown me off, as he so often did when we disagreed on something. Finally, it occurred to me that they were sitting in a car together.

"If you were consoling her why were you in her car?"

"Emma, think about it, we couldn't talk in the church. We might have been overheard."

"What you mean is that you couldn't kiss her in the church. Someone might see you," I sputtered.

"Emma, you're being irrational, and you're overreacting."

The more we talked the more I doubted my own mind. I kept going back to the picture in my head of them kissing. It seemed so obvious what he was doing. But now he was making me doubt what I had seen with my own eyes. He could do that. He had this amazing ability to convince you that you couldn't possibly have seen something that seemed so clear just minutes before. He was a master at making you question your own rational thought.

For days after this episode I went over and over what I had seen and what he said. My mind became more confused the more I thought about it. But the more I considered the situation the more I realized that it didn't matter anyway. Just like the first time, I realized that I was stuck. If he was having affairs with other women I still felt helpless to do anything about it.

I couldn't stand up to him, since he always managed to talk me down, and I still had the problem that if I decided to leave him where would I go, and how would I support a baby. I continued to feel that my only option was to try to preserve our relationship no matter how hard it became. I had to do this, not only for myself but for my baby.

Over the next two or three years I'm certain that he had affairs with several women. There was nothing as obvious as that night in the church parking lot. He was very skilled at keeping these liaisons hidden, but there were numerous subtle occurrences that made me suspect that something was going on. Just the way a woman was looking at him, or talking to him, made me realize that their relationship went well beyond just being friendly. When these little scenes occurred, I just looked away. I couldn't endure watching him draw these women into his trap.

Chapter 13

I Get a Job

When little Gary turned four, I decided it was time to get a job. As usual, we were having financial problems. Mel's salary as a teacher and minister barely covered our regular expenses, and he seemed to spend money with complete abandon. Every time he wanted to buy something, usually something we really couldn't afford, I tried to talk him out of it, or delay the purchase until our finances were better, but my pleading was to no avail. He would always come up with two or three good reasons that we needed it, or he would go on about how we had the money, that I was overreacting. Eventually, I gave up. On several occasions our debts grew so large that he had to ask his brother for money, and each time his brother gave him whatever he needed.

His brother was so good and so giving. Sometimes I wondered at the contrast between these two men who had the same mother and father. How could Mel and Edward be brothers. Edward was shy, didn't talk much, dedicated to work, devoted to his family, and uneasy around women. My husband, on the other hand, was a constant talker, unconcerned about how his actions might affect his family, and a real ladies man.

I felt awful taking so much money from his brother, but there was simply no way I could stop it. Mel and Edward would always talk about it as if it were just a loan, that we were going to pay the money back as soon as our financial situation turned around. Of course, that never happened, and Mel never paid back any of the "loans." I began to wonder if Mel was manipulating his brother in the same way that he manipulated other people and took advantage of women.

When little Gary entered Kindergarten, I took a job as a secretary in a law firm in Borger, about fifteen miles away from our house in Fritch. After I got over the initial adjustment period, and learned all the aspects of the job, I really liked the work and the daily routine. I soon realized that I had a knack for office and secretarial work. I was a fairly fast typist, and was good at organizational tasks. It was great getting out of the house, and I wondered how I had survived sitting at home for several years. I also liked my boss. He was very friendly and really appreciated my work.

Robert Herman, the attorney who owned the firm, had, like Mel, grown up in Borger. In fact, Robert's younger brother was in high school when Mel attended, although a couple of years older. After college Robert went to the University of Texas law school, and then came back to Borger to work in his father's firm. When I started working for the firm, Robert's father had just retired, and Robert had taken over the firm.

After a few months, I was on a first name basis with Robert, and he was inviting me out for drinks after work. At first our interactions were strictly about work-related matters, what might be thought of as normal socializing among people working together. But in a short time our socializing grew more and more personal. At first I was careful not to step over any lines that could be considered inappropriate for a married woman. But after an episode where I saw Mel being very friendly with another woman at church, I couldn't help but share my feelings with Robert.

I was so upset that day, and he somehow sensed that I was agitated about something. After trying to make conversation with me, and realizing how distracted I was, he finally asked me what was wrong. I broke down and told him about Mel's repeated infidelities, or suspected infidelities. Robert listened carefully and was very understanding.

After that initial discussion, I found myself sharing everything with Robert, and he always listened to my rants with deep sympathy. I soon felt closer to him than to Mel, but I didn't let anything other than conversation take place. I could tell that Robert wanted to become more intimate, and I could see the desire in his eyes, but I made it clear that we couldn't do anything inappropriate, and he respected those boundaries.

As things progressed, Mel grew ever more brazen with his "affairs" with other women. He seemed to develop an attitude that he could do anything he wanted and not suffer a single consequence. As he grew bolder in seeking out other women, I grew weaker and weaker in my attempts to keep Robert from initiating a closer relationship. Finally, on one evening after we had talked our way through several drinks, he made his move.

We were standing in the parking lot of the bar. He grabbed my arm and pressed me against the car, kissing me in a long embrace that I was simply powerless to resist. I felt awful and wonderful all at the same time. I felt that I had to stop what we were doing. I kept telling myself that I couldn't let this happen. At the same time I felt like it was the most wonderful feeling in the world.

After he let me go, and I got into my car, I thought I was going to be sick. How could I do this when I was married and had a small child? But I felt so alienated from Mel. He had no thought about my feelings, about what he was putting me through constantly. I desperately needed the support of someone, and Robert, so tender and understanding, gave me the emotional foundation and lift that I wasn't getting at home with Mel.

The very next day, just before lunch, Robert announced that we were closing the office for the afternoon. "You and I have plans," he said, leaning over my desk. I was afraid to ask what he had in mind, so I followed his commands, letting him take control. When he said he was ready to go, I simply placed the cover over my typewriter, picked up my purse, and followed him to his car. He drove us directly to his house. I had never been there before, and as we pulled into the driveway, I couldn't wait to find out what his house looked like on the inside. I felt like I was discovering something very intimate about this man.

When we went in, I have to say I was very impressed. For a single man, he had made some effort to make the place feel cozy and comfortable. He clearly had a good eye for decorating and had arranged things tastefully. At the same time, I couldn't find any trace of his own personality. There didn't seem to be anything unique or personal. I couldn't find a single family photograph anywhere. All the furniture, the pictures on the wall, and the decorations, looked like he had selected them from a magazine advertisement for a furniture store.

All of a sudden I felt this sinking feeling, a fear that maybe he decorated this way to impress women, that this house was his idea of how a woman would decorate. I wondered how many other women he had brought here, and I couldn't help but ask myself, was I just another in a long line of conquests.

I could certainly imagine a lot of women being interested in him. He was certainly attractive, he was a successful lawyer with a good income, and he was willing to listen to women talk about their problems and complaints. I had certainly wailed and whimpered at length about all my grievances. All these thoughts, running rapidly through my mind, were certainly disconcerting. But then I shook myself, and banished these troubling ideas from my head. After all, I was the one about to commit adultery, not him. How could I possibly question his motives?

It wasn't long before we were in bed together. It was wonderful, and nothing like sex with Mel. The feeling of being close with Robert was so completely different. Mel was aggressive, and sometimes even viciously brutal. He always demanded total obedience, always pushing or shoving me into the position he wanted. He rarely looked into my eyes, and if he did it was anything but a look of love.

Robert was the opposite, gently touching me, asking me how this or that touch felt, lightly stroking my breasts, my hips, and my inner thighs. He was large and muscular, but it seemed as if he had been able to train his large frame to control every movement in order to bring about just the right force and pressure on my body. For the first time in my life, I actually enjoyed the intimacy and the physicality of sex with complete abandon. I remember thinking to myself after we had finished making love, "so this is what everyone gets so excited about."

Here I was, a woman of 26, already in my seventh year of marriage, with a five year old child, and only now was I enjoying the first satisfying sex of my life. I couldn't help but wonder how many other women out there were in the same situation. How many women have to wait even longer? How many women are never able to enjoy a satisfying sexual relationship?

After that first afternoon together, we somehow found a way to meet at his house two, or sometimes, three times a week. I was living a dream, and for the first time in my life I was truly happy. After about three months I knew what I wanted, and I decided to take action to get it. I wanted to be with Robert, and I didn't want to be with Mel. I reached a point that I simply couldn't stand to be in the same room, sometimes in the same house, with Mel.

That led me to take the boldest, the most independent action, I have ever taken in my life. I rented a small apartment in Borger, and as soon as I was settled into my new living space, I filed for divorce. The day I made the move I took little Gary to a babysitter and then drove to the house in Fritch. There, I waited for Mel to come home.

When he walked in the door he knew immediately that something was up. "I don't see Gary, Where is he?" he asked.

"At the babysitter."

"Why?"

"Because I want a divorce," I said, in a dry even tone.

He just stared at me. Mel was always quick to respond no matter what the situation was. He always had something to say. But not this time. I could tell he was trying to figure out how to manipulate the situation to his own advantage, but he couldn't seem to come up with a response that would work. I knew that all he could think about at this point was how to recover his control over me, his domination, but I wasn't going to let him have it. I was beyond his manipulation now.

Of course, as I anticipated, after we talked for just a few minutes, he grew very angry. His face turned bright red, and the pupils of his eyes seemed to grow larger and darker. As soon as he began to raise his voice, I told him that I was leaving. As I headed for the door, he stepped in front of me and blocked my path, but I had anticipated that he might do something like this and was prepared. I told him that I had to go pick up Gary from the babysitter, and, "since I thought that you might do something like this, I told her that if I didn't arrive by seven p.m. she was to call the police and have them come over here and see if I was all right. So you better let me go."

I could see his fist clench, and I could tell that he wanted to hit me so much that he could taste it, but my threat stopped him. He knew that, for now, he had been out-maneuvered. He pivoted around, marched out of the room, and slammed the bedroom door. I left immediately.

Chapter 14

Nothing Ever Goes The Way You Think It Will

The next day I met Robert at his house late in the afternoon. I waited until after we made love, and then I told him what I had done. I covered all the details, telling him that I had rented an apartment, filed for a divorce, and had already told Mel that I was leaving him for good. He immediately got out of bed, put a robe on, and walked to the window. I was a little confused. I thought he would be ecstatic, but his response was very measured. He seemed distant in a way I had never experienced before. At first, he just stood at the window, looking out over the yard, not saying a thing.

I waited, thinking he would say something, but after a few minutes I couldn't stand the silence any longer. "I thought you would be excited for me, and glad that we can be together even more," I said, as I sat up in bed and tried to get a glimpse of his face. But he was turned away from me, still staring out the window.

After a long pause he responded. "I know you wanted to get away from him, and it's probably a good thing, but divorce can be complicated. It can be messy. I want to support you, but I don't want to get too involved. Do you understand? I can't get too involved. I have a reputation in town, and if things get too messy it might have an impact on my law practice."

"I understand," I said hesitantly. "I didn't think about that. You're right. I have to make sure that the divorce doesn't involve you."

He turned away from the window, looking at me with deep concern. "I don't think we should move too fast on our relationship. We can continue to get together as we're doing now, but we have to be very careful." He paused, thinking things through. "I don't want Mel finding out what we're doing. That could really complicate matters and make your divorce much more difficult."

"You're right, I understand," I said. "I guess I didn't think everything over completely. You're right, I do need to be careful and keep you completely out of it. Knowing Mel, it could be a very messy divorce. He can be very vindictive."

There was silence between us for several minutes after that. It was getting dark outside, and there were no lights on in the room. I began to realize that simply leaving Mel and turning to Robert wasn't so straightforward. I could see that Robert had reservations about the situation, and how could I blame him.

"I hope you're not mad at me," I asked tentatively. "I just had to get out. I couldn't stand to stay with him."

"No, I'm not mad" Robert replied. "Let's just not get ahead of ourselves."

Of course, absolutely nothing went the way I had expected. A week later Robert told me that he didn't think it was a good idea for me to continue working at his law practice. He put in a call to one of the other lawyers in town and got me a job there. Within a few days I was working for the new firm.

Then, an even bigger complication blew up in my face. Just one month after I walked out of my marriage, I found out I was pregnant. Although I had tried to take every precaution, somehow, I was pregnant, and what made it even worse, I wasn't sure who the father was. Mel had demanded that we have sex a couple of times in the weeks before I left, and so I couldn't be certain who fathered my baby.

Things started to get very complicated with little Gary as well. I thought that he would adjust once I had him settled into the new apartment. I thought he would get used to periodic visits with his dad, but he didn't. He cried constantly and begged to see his dad every day. I tried everything I could think of to help him settle into his new routine, but nothing worked.

Every week I told him that he would see his father on the weekend, but nothing could distract him from his distress. He wanted his dad, and nothing would make him happy until his dad was there. On one occasion he became so distraught that I eventually gave in and called Mel. Gary begged to let his father come over, and I eventually gave in to his pleas. Of course, Mel took advantage of the situation and wound up convincing me to let him stay over that night. "Gary needs his father tonight," he said. What could I do but give in to Gary's pleas and Mel's manipulations.

From then on I knew that I had a major problem with my son. As I've pointed out already, Mel could make anyone worship him. He was great at making people think he was essential to their very existence, that somehow they couldn't live without him. I now realized that my son was no different. Little Gary simply lived to be with his father.

I know that most young children need both parents, but I had always thought that kids generally were closer to their moms, and that usually, in the case of a divorce, living with their mother was clearly the best option. But Mel had somehow brainwashed this gentle five year old boy into believing that he couldn't live without his dad.

After I discovered that I was pregnant, I had to decide what to do. For at least a week I didn't tell anyone. Night and day I tried to think through what my best options were. I must have considered dozens of scenarios, but none seemed great. In fact, most didn't even seem viable.

I finally had no other choice but to tell Robert. He had been so understanding in the past, and that's what I expected from him now. But the conversation didn't go well. He got mad almost immediately. He then accused me of trying to trap him into marriage. I was shocked that he could think such a thing, and I tried to convince him that I would never think of doing anything like that. I tried to reason with him and explain that while I was going through a divorce the last thing I wanted was to be pregnant at the same time. I kept repeating that trapping him was the furthest thing from my mind, but he didn't believe me. He then asked me strait out if I knew who the father was. I had to admit that I wasn't certain.

That was it. That was his way out. "Maybe it's better if we don't see each other while everything is so up in the air. Things are just way too complicated." I left in tears. Less than six weeks after I had walked out on Mel, I was now pregnant, dealing with a son bereft without his father, and without the man who had given me the courage to initiate leaving Mel in the first place.

The night that Robert put an end to our relationship I felt suicidal. After I got little Gary to sleep, I seriously considered ending it all and killing myself. I sat on the side of my bed and stared at a bottle of sleeping pills, wondering if they would do the trick. For several hours I sat there on the side of my bed and contemplated what it would be like just to drift off into oblivion. I think the only thing that kept me from going forward with it was the fear that little Gary would discover my lifeless body in the morning.

For the next several months I tried to continue on my course. I wanted so desperately to leave Mel behind. I kept telling myself that I could do it, that I could live on my own. But my son continued to be terribly upset without his father, and I knew that it was just a matter of time before I would have to give him up and let him live with Mel. To complicate matters even more, I was starting to show. Soon everyone would know that I was pregnant. When I was forced to quit work, how would I support myself and two children? I remembered how difficult it had been in the first months after Gary was born. How could I possibly do it again by myself?

I finally gave in and asked Mel if we could reconcile and get back together. It made me sick to my stomach to consider going back to him, but I kept saying to myself that at least I won't loose my son. I knew that if I was forced to let Mel take Gary Mel wouldn't let me see him, and I just couldn't even imagine not being able to see my son.

Of course, when we met to discuss the possibility of renewing our marriage, he went on and on about how I had hurt him terribly. After he grew tired of haranguing me on that subject, he switched to talking about how I had hurt our son and how he couldn't understand how a mother could do that to a little boy. Then he switched subjects again and went on for some time about how I had been selfish and thoughtless.

After a couple of hours of this constant barrage I thought he would never stop talking about how terrible I was. I just sat there and took it. What else could I do? Eventually, after he felt that he had beaten me down enough, he agreed to take me back. He saw the reconciliation as a big victory, and he now knew that his son would reject me and choose him if I tried to divorce again.

That night, in order to "renew our marriage," as he put it, he forced me to undress in front of him while he stared at me. Then, when I was standing there naked, he walked up to me and slapped me a couple of times. He then spun me around and pushed me down on the floor, ordering me to get down on my hands and knees. He then thrust himself into me as hard as he could. I just closed my eyes and waited for it to be over.

I gave birth to my second son a few months later. We named him Marc. He was very different from little Gary. He was much more active and independent, even as a baby. He sometimes seemed to ignore me and live in his own world. I wondered at times if I had somehow damaged his brains during pregnancy since I was going through such turmoil. I even asked my doctor about it when I took him for his one year check-up. He assured me that I had done nothing wrong, but I couldn't help but harbor doubts.

I soon had other things to worry about. Mel had accumulated such staggering debts that even his brother wasn't able to cover them all. Store owners in the town soon stopped allowing us to shop in their stores, and some were extremely hostile. There had also been a couple of problems with women in the church. One had contacted the bishop and had threatened legal action against Mel. Eventually, she backed down and decided that it was best to let the matter drop. I'm sure she was worried, like several other women victimized by Mel, that her reputation would be destroyed. Her husband had left her over the affair, and my guess is that going through a divorce was trauma enough for her.

There was also another incident with a high school girl. This time the father was so irate that he threatened to kill Mel, but apparently his daughter pleaded with him to let it go. She was afraid her boyfriend would find out. So Mel continued to get away with his seductions of vulnerable women and girls. At least this time, the bishop refused to appoint him to another church. His career as a minister was now over. With bill collectors beating at the door, and aggrieved women threatening legal action, we were forced to leave Fritch and move. Finally, after months of looking, Mel got a job in a god-forsaken, dust-covered town called Morton, some ninety or so miles west of Lubbock, Texas.

I had felt isolated at times in Fritch, but nothing like this. At least in Fritch I was only fifteen or so miles from Borger. The city of Borger was not exactly a metropolis, but at least it was a fairly large town of some 20,000 people, and had some good shops. Amarillo, a fairly large city, was only an hour's drive away. Morton was even smaller than Fritch, and the only place to find a decent department store was a good two hours drive away in Lubbock.

I hated Morton in almost every way. Since we weren't exactly rolling in cash, we had to take a small adobe home that I thought was probably one of the ugliest houses I had ever seen. Mel went on about how neat it was to live in an adobe home. "It's so well insulated," he kept repeating. I knew he really didn't care how insulated it was. It was just Mel doing his usual thing and spinning our deplorable situation as much better than it was.

To make matters worse, the countryside around Morton was dry, flat, and almost totally barren of trees. It seemed so lonely and desolate when I drove out of town on my occasional forays into Lubbock. To me, it seemed that the people living in the town seemed stunted by both the lack of stimulation and the barrenness of their surroundings.

I tried to make the best of my situation and devote my attention to raising two active boys. More and more, as the weeks and months of my miserable life passed, I realized that I was going through the motions of my daily routine. As I went through the process of getting the kids ready for school, going to the grocery store, cleaning the house, and the hundreds of other jobs of a busy mother, I often felt like my mind and my body were disconnected. I was becoming increasingly alienated from my existence.

Sometimes, when I was sitting with my friends, complaining about our husbands, or talking about what our children were doing, I could feel myself disconnect from the group. It was almost like my spirit began to separate from my body and gradually rise up. It felt like I was hovering above the group, looking down on my friends, and my own body. I became this invisible ghost studying these strange creatures.

Sometimes, I almost felt like I was becoming this soul without a will. I didn't really care one way or another what was being said, or what people thought. I just wanted to observe each of these creatures and the life they were living. I was like an anthropologist scientifically studying some strange tribe in some remote corner of the planet.

I began to realize that we indeed were a strange tribe. There was no real reason that we exhibited these characteristics. The traits we all displayed and practiced on a daily basis were developed through a varied combination of assumptions, traditions that we weren't even aware of, and conditions that we didn't understand. Amazingly, we all thought that the way we were, the things we did, the beliefs we held so fervently, were all logical results of rules dictated by unalterable universal laws

When I had these sensations of becoming a disembodied entity hovering over the people around me, it was like I had escaped a cave and was seeing a completely different world out in the sunshine. When I looked back at my friends, the people still back in the cave, I didn't know how to tell them that they were trapped in a dark cave. Even though I felt like I was seeing the world outside the cave, I didn't know how to live out there. I kept feeling that I had no other choice but to return to the cave.

There were times that I tried to tell a friend about my feelings of disconnection, my alienation from the limited world in rural Texas, but I couldn't seem to discover a way to communicate these ideas. My friends were often disgruntled themselves, and wanted to change things about their lives, but most of them had never gone through the process of being torn out of their comfortable worlds and forced to observe society as an outsider. They were caught in a trap that they didn't even realize was a trap.

I now see that I was developing the penetrating gaze, the special vision of the artist, but I hadn't yet found my medium. In this circumscribed world, no one said to me - "have you thought about becoming an artist? Maybe you should try painting." At that point, I knew so little about art. Sure, I was an ardent book reader, and the books I had read had exposed me to the arts. But there's a big difference between seeing reproductions of paintings in books, and seeing real works of art in a gallery or museum. Soon, that was about to change.

Chapter 15

Discovering Art

Then, something extraordinary happened, something that, quite possibly, saved my life. It was 1963. Gary was twelve and Marc was seven. By this time I was just trying to make it from one day to the next, trying to take care of the kids, and keep myself from falling into a deep depression.

Mel had been selected to go to a special teacher's conference in Chicago for a week. He asked me if I would like to leave the kids with his mother and spend the week with him. I really wasn't at all excited about spending time with him, but I finally decided that it would be good to get away. I had never seen Chicago, so I thought it might be interesting. Six weeks later we loaded up the car and headed for the airport.

During the day Mel was busy with the various activities at his conference, so I looked for things to do. At first, I did the typical tourist activities. I had never been to a city as large as Chicago before. In fact, I had rarely even been in a big city. Lubbock and Amarillo hardly counted. Let's face it, both of those cities are really overgrown small towns. El Paso, where I spent most of my teenage years, was a little larger, but it too had few of the cultural opportunities of cities like New York and Chicago. Like most Americans living in the West in that period, the vast majority of my experiences came from life on farms and in small towns.

Since you're a New York girl you probably don't understand this, but not all cities are created equal. Unless you are living in a mega-city like New York, or Paris, or London, smaller cities don't necessarily have all the cultural amenities we usually associate with larger urban areas.

Even smaller European cities have a decided advantage over cities in the American West. If, for instance, you live in a German city, and you realize that your city is missing something important, you have options. Let's say, for the sake of argument, that you're interested in Cubist art, and the museum in your city doesn't have a good Cubist collection. The solution is simple. Just jump on a train and go to a neighboring city, usually no more than a couple of hours away, that has a museum with a better Cubist collection.

In the Western part of the United States, cities are separated by much greater distances. If the city where you reside doesn't have something you need, a city that does may be much further away. What makes the problem even worse in the United States is the simple fact that American cities are much younger when compared to those in Europe. Regrettably, American cultural institutions, especially those in the heartland, tend to have a lot of deficiencies when it comes to art and culture.

Now, I was in a truly big city, and I wanted to explore. On the third day of our visit, I decided to spend a couple of hours at the Chicago Institute of Art. I arrived late in the morning, after a late breakfast at the hotel. I had planned to spend a couple of hours there before venturing on for some shopping downtown. I wound up staying until a courteous security guard informed me that the museum was closing.

I was simply stunned with what I saw. I walked into a large gallery of Abstract Expressionist paintings and my life changed in the space of five minutes. Here on the walls were huge canvases by Jackson Pollock, William de Kooning, Mark Rothko, Robert Motherwell, and a number of other giants of the art movement that swept the New York art scene in the 1940s and 1950s.

Of course, being the type of person who tried to stay up on various intellectual currents, I had heard of this art movement. In fact, I think I might have even read a couple of magazine articles about some of these artists. But before walking into this gallery I viewed modern art as strange, a little quirky, and certainly not relevant to my life. Modern art seemed the province of weird men in berets, living in a garret in Paris. What little I knew of their paintings, seen in magazine and book reproductions, seemed to be the work of mad men trying to be intellectuals.

When I walked into that spacious gallery, and saw these huge canvases, I was absolutely shocked by the overwhelming impact these paintings imparted. I felt like I was looking into another world. I was still totally confused by these modern works of art. They seemed so different from what I knew, or thought I knew, art to be. These paintings exuded some sort of power, some sort of mystical effect. They were absolutely mesmerizing. The colors were vivid and electric, and the slashing brushstrokes so powerful and violent. I actually felt dizzy literally minutes after walking into this room.

I loved the swirls and sweeps of Pollock's dancing lines, the thick brushstrokes of Kline's wonderful black and white paintings, and the seemingly translucent fields of red and yellow in Rothko's canvases. On that first day I must have spent at least an hour deeply transfixed by each of these three artists.

Then I moved into the next room of the museum and discovered the paintings of Helen Frankenthaler, Grace Hartigan, and Joan Mitchell. Frankenthaler's vast stain paintings, so transparent and unearthly, and Mitchell's chaotic fields of slashing and churning brushstrokes, simply took my breath away. I couldn't believe that women - not men - women were creating such original, such violent, such beautiful, paintings. How could a woman possibly be an artist, an artist who had paintings in a museum like this? How could a woman learn about this strange, bewildering art, and then somehow create original styles that looked like nothing I had ever seen before? Look what these women had done, what they had accomplished, and here I was, already in my thirties, having accomplished nothing.

I spent the next three days in this museum, or to be more exact, I spent the nexts three days in the three rooms of the Art Institute that featured Abstract Expressionist art. I was standing on the steps when the guards opened the door, and I left when the guards ushered me out. Mel thought I had gone crazy, which was probably not a totally inaccurate description. He kept asking me why I wasn't taking advantage of my time in Chicago to do other things. I didn't even try to explain. I just told him, "I'm going back to the museum."

Of course, I now realize that at that time, the spring of 1963, Abstract Expressionism was, at least in New York, already passé. The art world had already moved on to Pop Art, Minimalism, and other assorted isms. But at that point, I didn't even understand what Picasso had done in 1910, much less what the Abstract Expressionists had done in the 1950s. I was way behind, and had a lot of catching up to do.

When we got back to Texas, I headed strait to the local public library to look for books on modern art. When I realized that the little library in Morton had practically nothing on Abstract Expressionism, and, in fact, had very little on modern art, I jumped in the car and drove to the Lubbock Public Library. Within just a couple of months I had read almost every book the library possessed on the subject.

Soon, I was in another world. Mel and the kids thought I was starting to become a little weird, and I have to admit that, to an outside observer, I must have seemed very strange at this juncture. There were times that Mel, or one of the kids, would say something to me, and I wouldn't hear a word. Often, at dinner, I was completely unaware of what was being said, or what my family was doing. There were times that one of the kids would have to yell at me to get my attention.

From the time I got up in the morning until I went to sleep at night, I was totally immersed in the world of modern art, and I was becoming increasingly upset that I had access to so little contemporary art in Texas. Lubbock didn't even have a small museum like most cities possess. I wanted so much to see more of what I had seen in Chicago.

About three months after my return from Chicago I decided that I wanted to try my hand at painting. I had no idea if I had any talent at all, I just knew that I had to try. Some feeling in me wanted to connect to a strong creative urge stirring within me.

After some searching, I found an artist in a neighboring town who was willing to give me private lessons. She worked in her barn during the summer and in a small, sparsely heated room during the winter. I wanted to go every day, but she laughed, and suggested that we meet once a week. I loved it from the minute we started. She introduced me to drawing, mixing paints, perspective, and so many other aspects of the craft of painting. Although her paintings were fairly conventional - the typical landscapes, drawings of pretty flowers in vases, or cute children playing in the garden - at least I learned basic techniques from her. She was really what you would call a folk artist, but that was the only kind of artist that existed in remote, rural Texas.

After each lesson, I quickly returned home and went right to work, practicing what she had taught me. I spent hours in the makeshift studio I made out of our spare bedroom. Soon the family learned that if they needed me for some reason they knew where to find me.

Mel seriously began to wonder what was going on with me. About six months into my new obsession, after a dinner where I had been especially preoccupied, he asked me if I was getting a little too carried away. He suggested that maybe I should take a break and do something else for awhile.

He also commented that the kids were starting to feel ignored. "You need to remember that you are a mother, and your kids need your attention."

My blood pressure must have doubled in less than five seconds. We were in the kitchen, and I was standing at the sink. I spun around and took a step toward him. My face turned three shades of crimson, and I must have looked like I was about to commit murder, because he jerked back and looked totally startled.

"You have a lot of gall," I spit out. "For all these years, while you sit on your ass reading the newspaper, or watching television, or chasing other women, I'm the one who feeds those kids, helps them with their homework, takes them to all their appointments, makes sure they make it to school, and takes care of them when they get sick. What the hell have you been doing," I yelled.

"You waltz in here after I have dinner on the table, pat your little darling kids on the head, ask them how their day was, and think you've done your duty. Well let me tell you something. If you think your kids are being ignored, there's a simple solution. You can spend more time with them. Let me know if you want to take them to school tomorrow. By the way, Marc has a doctor's appointment tomorrow afternoon. You are more than welcome to take him."

Mel just walked away. He was shaking his head, and I could tell that he was thinking his usual thoughts after I got mad about something. Anytime I got angry he would laugh and say to the kids, "Your mother is having one of her 'crazy female' moments." Or another one of his favorite lines was, "Oh no, female hormones are kicking in." Every time he made one of these comments the boys would laugh like it was one of the funniest jokes they had ever heard.

Of course, the kids heard my yelling. I felt like a terrible mother and a bad wife. Although my marriage was unhappy, and I found myself irritated by something Mel did, or did not do, on a daily basis, I made a point of trying to avoid arguing, or raising my voice in front of the kids. Although I sometimes fell short and yelled in spite of my effort to hold back, at least at this time, I think they thought we were a fairly normal couple.

As I consoled the kids, and told them that everything was fine, there was one thought that stayed with me that evening. I was not going to give up art. It was the one thing that got me out of bed in the morning, and the one thing that made me feel like I might just do something that could have an impact in this crazy world. The family would just have to adjust. I had bent over backwards to do things for them. Maybe, it was time that they had to do a little bending for me.

Of course, I should have known better. Children and, regrettably, most husbands, don't adjust to accommodate their mothers or wives. Children want their mother to be nothing but a mother. She's not supposed to be an artist, or anything else for that matter. Her job is to be there for them no matter what, and when she isn't they hold it against her.

By this point, the Feminist movement was taking off in America. On the television news I had watched with fascination as women on college campuses protested unfair treatment by men in a patriarchal society. But I saw little evidence of that sort of change in Texas. Maybe it was happening on the campuses, and maybe things were different on the coasts, but the American heartland was still entrenched in good-old conservative values. And those values didn't look kindly on uppity women deciding to become artists, especially contemporary artists.

Maybe we've made a lot of progress since the time I was raising my kids, but there's a long way to go. Women may have careers now, but they are still expected to be a mother first and foremost. Most people I know now espouse the values of Feminism until their own mothers decide to become independent. Then they change their tune in a heartbeat. Sure, other women can be independent, but they want their own mother to be as traditional as apple pie.

Husbands are even worse. A wife has to be available for sex anytime the husband wants it, but still remain virginal and pure, always willing to have dinner on the table, and take care of the kids. My grandkids are telling me that things are changing, but I don't see much evidence of it. Most of the changes I see are fairly incremental and superficial. A lot of young women today see utopia right around the corner. I'm afraid that, with my few years left, I won't see it.

Needless to say, I continued to work on my art, and - according to my family - grew more and more remote. I felt that I continued to lavish energy and time on them as I always had. Yet, they only seemed to notice the times that I wasn't there for them.

Gary, who had been such a darling little boy, became moody and distant as he grew into his teenage years. He began to answer my questions with shrugs, or grunts, or one word answers. He often spent the time until his dad came home from work locked away in his room.

I remember one afternoon when he walked in from school. I asked him how his day had gone. He replied, "What do you care, the only thing that really matters to you is your art." I was stunned, and I just stood there dumbfounded, totally unable to respond.

Marc was no better. He had always been a little more independent, and I think that he simply wrote me off as a mother who didn't care. His attitude was simply - if she doesn't care I don't either. During one epic battle over some trivial matter he yelled, "Just leave me alone, and go do one of your paintings."

I blamed a lot of this on Mel and his influence. As time went on, he found more and more ways to take little swipes at my interest in art. If I mentioned what I was working on with a particular painting, or that I planned to meet with my teacher, he would say, "There goes your mother again, doing her art thing."

At one point I tried to counter Mel's influence by trying to get the kids interested in doing some art themselves. On several occasions, I invited them into my studio to work alongside me. I suggested that they could make their own paintings, and I told them that they could use the watercolors or pastels and make any kind of picture they liked.

Gary reluctantly gave it a try on a couple of occasions. He sat down at a work table I had set up next to my easel, but each time he gave it a try he produced a drawing that was little better than a stick figure painting you might see in a first grade classroom. Of course, I raved about how good his drawing was to encourage his efforts. On one occasion, right after I had told him that he was off to a good start, he looked at his drawing and said, "This is stupid. I don't want to do this anymore." He then headed straight out the door to go outside and play baseball.

All my efforts with Marc were totally useless. I couldn't even get him in the studio. Every time I suggested that he join me, and try his hand at a drawing, he would immediately develop a strong interest in going outside to play ball, and usually Mel was more than willing to take the kids to the park for some baseball or basketball.

One thing I'll say about Mel, he was really good at playing with the kids. They loved to hear him say, "Let's head to the park for some basketball." During football season, before a game would come on television, he had the kids out in the back yard catching football passes.

Then, at halftime, they would run back out there again. They would run pass plays that Mel taught them. Sometimes, he would tell tall tales about when he was a football coach and the success of the plays he would have his team run.

I often thought that the reason Mel was so good playing sports with the kids was that he was really just a kid himself. I sometimes felt that he had the maturity of a fourteen year old, but that was probably just jealousy on my part. I wanted so much to be able to connect with the kids the way Mel did, but I just wasn't able to do so. Of course, part of it was the simple fact that they were boys and naturally related to their father more. I often wonder what it would have been like to have had a girl to raise. Would she have connected more to me? I don't know.

Another point of contention between us was the fact that Mel didn't appreciate a lot of the subjects I chose to explore in my paintings. At one point I was trying to address certain issues related to the plight of women in society. Remember, these were the years that Feminism was in the news. That led me to incorporate nudes, both male and female, into some of my work.

Many of these nude figures were enveloped in a hazy, atmospheric landscape, or were partially covered in brushstrokes similar to those employed by De Kooning in his early 1950s paintings of women. Some of the nudes were even so obscure that it was difficult to make out the figure. I was using this visual context to explore the subjugation of women, but that didn't matter to Mel. When he saw a group of paintings I was putting together for a local show, I thought he was going to have a heart attack.

"You can't show those paintings," he blurted out. "What the hell do you think you're doing. What do you suppose the neighbors would think if they saw paintings like that."

"I frankly don't care," I replied.

"You wouldn't," he yelled, and stormed out.

The kids didn't say much about these paintings, but I could tell they were embarrassed by them. At one point I had a painting hanging in the living room. It was one of my murky nude paintings, where you could just make out a figure among an explosion of colorful brushstrokes.

131

When Marc was having some friends over, he asked if I could take it down while they were here.

I was so mad that I felt like hanging my nudes on every wall of the house. But, of course, I complied and took it down. After that I never hung another painting in the house. I always kept them locked away in my studio.

When I moved onto abstract work, that also generated negative and ridiculously sarcastic comments. Mel kept talking about my "scratch and splatter" paintings, as he had nicknamed them, and the kids laughed hysterically almost every time he said it. If Mel and I went to a party I was always instructed that, under no circumstances was I to talk about my art.

At one dinner party the wife of another teacher had seen several of my paintings when I had her and a couple of other friends over to the house. She and I were in a book club together, and it was my turn to host. After refreshments, and our discussion about the assigned book, I invited the group into my studio to see the paintings I was working on at the time.

When she and her husband met Mel and I for dinner, maybe a month later, she asked me about one of the paintings that I had on my easel at the time of the book group meeting. It was a nude, and she wanted to know if I used models. When I started to answer her question Mel gave me a solid kick under the table. He clearly didn't want me to talk about anything having to do with naked bodies, or how one goes about painting them.

Of course, the sad thing about this episode, and several other similar social occasions, was that Mel might have been right. In backward Morton, Texas, where probably a vast majority of the population had never darkened the door of an art museum, it's my guess that the general perception was that people who talked about art, much less actually created art, were a little strange.

This was a very conservative area of the country. It was also in the middle of the Bible Belt. Many people had major issues with nude art. Who knows what my friend thought. Even if she was truly interested in my art, who knows what her husband thought about my unusual proclivities. What did that couple talk about on the way home after our dinner? For all I know they were laughing about how weird I was. Or, maybe they were totally scandalized by my paintings. It was quite possible they could have been having a discussion about how my interest in painting nude bodies was very sinful.

Chapter 16

My First Art Show

After several years of working on honing my skills as a painter, I finally found the courage to submit one of my paintings to a juried group show. The judge was a respected professor of art from the University of Texas. He had been brought to Lubbock by a local arts group in the city that tried to put on art shows featuring local talent once or twice a year. When I read about this show in the newspaper, I was so excited by the possibility of displaying my work in an actual exhibit. At the same time, I worried that I would be rejected. If I didn't make it into the show, I thought to myself, it would then be obvious that I had no talent. At several points I almost backed out, thinking that I wasn't ready, wondering if I should continue to work on my technique more before I took the plunge.

After much vacillation I finally entered one of my "scratch and splatter" paintings, as Mel described it. As it turned out, my painting was not only accepted, it won the award for the best painting in the show. My family couldn't believe it. I think Mel was completely baffled at first, but he soon wrote it off as just another example of how weird all artists are. "Of course it was accepted into the show," he said. "You artists always go for that weird stuff, and your painting certainly classifies as weird." The kids got a great laugh out of that comment.

At the awards ceremony, that my family refused to attend, I asked the professor, who had served as the juror for the exhibit, what he thought I should do to further my career. He suggested taking up a course of study with an artist by the name of Don Holt, who had recently arrived in Lubbock to give a series of guest lectures. He was also scheduled to serve a term as an artist-in-residence at Texas Tech University. He explained that Don Holt was an esteemed artist from Santa Fe and was also a professor at the University of New Mexico. He was known as a great teacher. His students loved him, and he had helped launch the careers of a number of artists. He offered to call him and recommend me. I was elated.

The only problem was that I couldn't figure out how I could possibly make it from Morton to Lubbock to study with a professor in a formal college program? Driving two hours there and two hours back several days a week seemed more than I could reasonably handle and more than what my family would tolerate. When I finally reached Professor Holt by phone, I explained that I wanted to study with him, but didn't know how I could travel back and forth from my home to Lubbock.

He suggested that I should make arrangements to stay in Lubbock for at least part of the week. He proposed that I attend his lectures by auditing his classes. That would give me more flexibility if I needed to occasionally return home. I didn't have to formally enroll. In addition to the lectures, I could work with him privately. I was so excited by the possibility of working with a well-known artist, but I worried that I wouldn't be able to do it.

When I brought up this idea with Mel, he absolutely refused to agree to it. "Are you absolutely crazy," he said. "Are you going to simply abandon your kids for several months so you can pursue some wild idea of studying weird art."

I was devastated, and for several weeks I fell into a deep depression. For the first time since I had started my quest to become an artist I didn't paint a single brushstroke for more than four weeks. I finally realized that I couldn't go on this way. I would die if I didn't find a way of pursuing my course as an artist. I confronted Mel and said that, no matter what, I was going through with this. If he didn't accept my decision I would file for divorce. He had no choice but to let me go.

I left for Lubbock early in September, 1967. Gary was sixteen and Marc was eleven. Surely, they were old enough to take care of themselves for a few months. If there was a problem, I could easily make it home in just a couple of hours. But in the days before I left both my children acted as though I was the worst mom in the history of humanity.

Of course, being a mom, I felt really guilty. I kept asking myself all the typical questions. Was I selfish? Was I a terrible mother? Was there any other way to pursue the study of art and not leave the children?

I don't know how I made it through those torturous days before I left, but I stuck to my plan. I loaded up the car on a Sunday afternoon while Mel and the kids sulked and refused to talk to me. When I was finally ready to go, I tried to give the kids a hug. They just stood there stiff as a board. I cried all the way to Lubbock.

When I got there, I moved my things into a tiny studio apartment not far from the campus. Don had helped me locate an apartment through the campus housing office. Although I wasn't officially a student, he had pulled some strings to get them to help me find a place to stay.

That first week was wonderful and awful at the same time. I felt so guilty about abandoning the kids. I must have berated myself for being a bad mother about once an hour. I kept thinking about how they looked at me as I was leaving, and every time I visualized it in my head I could actually feel a twinge of pain in my chest.

On the other hand, starting my art studies was an amazing thrill. Early on Monday morning I met Don in his office. I immediately liked him. He was a handsome man, about fifty years of age. He had a nice tan, and his hair hung down loosely to his shoulders. This was the era of the hippies, and I thought that Don, although much older than most hippies in those days, certainly looked like he could hang out with them and not look out of place. I also was immediately aware of how different he was from Mel, who always kept his hair short and trim. I was so impressed by how relaxed Don was. He had an easy manner and exuded a quiet confidence.

After we talked for a half hour or so about the course of study he recommended he then asked to see my work. I was so nervous that I could barely open the portfolio of small paintings and drawings I had brought to show him. I was sure that he would think they were awful, and I prayed that he didn't change his mind about allowing me to study with him. I had this picture in my mind of him being totally turned off by my work, but his reaction was amazingly positive. As he turned the pages and studied several drawings, a few watercolors, and some pastels, he bobbed his head up and down affirmatively.

"Yes, yes," he said, "this is good. This drawing is excellent. Yes, I like this pastel. Very interesting. I like what you did here. You clearly have a good eye." I thought I was going to faint. I can still remember reaching out and grabbing his work table for stability as the room swirled around me.

The rest of the semester was simply a dream. It flew by so quickly, and I learned so much. Just working with Don was inspiring, and his lectures added tremendously to the experience. He obviously knew so much about the art of the twentieth century, and I needed that background desperately. Although I was much older than most of the other students in Don's class, I enjoyed interacting with the other budding artists. It was great to be a part of a community of people trying to become artists, all truly serious about what they were doing. I also discovered that many of them were like me. Most had grown up somewhere in the area, had somehow discovered art, and wanted to pursue it in a serious way. But there were few opportunities for artists in West Texas. Study at the University, limited as it was, provided their only option.

My private lessons with Don were extremely helpful. I would bring in what I was working on and have him take a look at it. He always examined each of my pieces very carefully for several minutes. Usually, he identified one aspect of the painting or drawing for comment. He always began with a positive remark, but then suggested something he thought I could do to improve the picture.

A typical evaluation might start with, "Yes, yes, I like your fluid brushstrokes here and here, very nice, very strong, but it seems to me that you need to carry these ideas into this area of the canvas. It seems that the painting will feel incomplete if you don't." Then he would notice something in another area of the canvas and make similar comments.

After reviewing the canvas I was working on at the time he would then suggest an exercise of some kind. "Since you're working in this way, why don't you try this." It might be a simple drawing that he would ask me to try in several different ways, or a technique designed to bring about a certain effect. After every lesson I would run back to my tiny studio apartment and go right to work. I couldn't wait to try everything he suggested.

Often, on lesson days, that usually took place two and sometimes three times a week, I would spend five of six hours following through on his suggestions. I sometimes skipped meals, and I often lost track of the time. I was so absorbed in the ideas that he opened up for me that I often couldn't get them out of my head. Even when I finally turned away from my easel, I couldn't think of anything else. All I wanted to do was return to that easel. Time lost its usual boundaries and evolved into a fluid entity moving at incredible speed when I was absorbed in my work.

I didn't return home until Thanksgiving. Although I had told Mel and the kids that I could come home anytime they needed me, they had managed just fine without me. I arrived home on Tuesday evening two days before Thanksgiving. When I walked in the door, suitcases in hand, Mel was sprawled out on the living room couch watching television. I said hello, and then I quickly walked to the bedroom. There I started packing for our trip. We had decided to travel to Borger to have Thanksgiving with the rest of Mel's family.

After awhile, Mel appeared and leaned against the side of the bedroom door. "So, have you learned all you need to know about modern art?"

"Not really," I replied. I knew he was just trying to get a rise out of me, to irritate me if he could, and I was trying my best to resist taking the bait.

He waited a minute, watching me pick through my clothes. I continued to ignore him, and I'm sure that just inspired him all the more to try to figure out a way to harass me. "I have a question for you," he began. "How can you spend an entire semester studying art that any five year old could create in an afternoon session of her kindergarten class?"

I turned around and stared at him, wondering how I had managed to survive living with this cretin for all these years. How had I somehow raised two children with this person? It also struck me as ironic that this statement was coming from him. He had been the one that had always prided himself on how smart he was, how well educated he was. He was the one who was always telling me how most people were so uneducated and so unsophisticated. Yet, here he was, spewing out cliche statements that even most Philistines would be embarrassed to make.

But I wasn't about to engage with him in this stupid conversation. "I really don't want to talk about it right now. I have a lot to do to get everything ready for our trip. Don't you have stuff to pack?" He walked out and returned to his television show.

The next morning we loaded the car and made the drive to Borger. The kids, sitting in the back seat bugging each other for most of the trip, seemed totally uninterested in talking with me, or catching up after almost three months apart. Mel wasn't interested in talking either, which was actually a blessing.

When we got back on Sunday I quickly packed my car and headed for Lubbock, ready to get back to work, and thankful that this dreaded holiday was over. There were three more weeks left in the semester, and I wanted to make the most of them. Once I was back in the routine my work went very well. It seemed like all the experiments, all the exercises, all the lectures, and all the time staring at my canvases over the course of the semester, were paying off. I finally felt I was getting somewhere, and I was actually beginning to break through, that at least a few of the pieces I was creating were actually respectable.

At the end of the semester, when Don was packing his things, and preparing to return to Santa Fe, I was in tears. I felt like I was only getting started, that I needed to spend a lot more time under his tutelage. I remember not being able to work and wondering how I could go on with my art. One afternoon, at a particular low point, unable to even pick up a brush, I walked over to his office. I explained my desperation, and my feeling that I needed to continue my studies with him. I also explained that I didn't want to go home to my husband. This wasn't the first time that I had confided in him and explained that my marriage was very troubled.

After listening to me pour out my feelings for probably close to an hour, he said, "Emma, you must realize that you are at a crossroads, and you need to make a decision. If you go back to your husband, I doubt that you will be able to pursue your desire to become an artist in any meaningful way. But you can't stay in Lubbock either. The art scene here is non-existent. West Texas has nothing to offer a serious contemporary artist. That is the sad but obvious reality."

He paused at this point, took a deep breath, and looked strait at me. "You do have an alternative, but it might be very difficult for you to even imagine following through on it. You could consider coming to Santa Fe and continuing to work with me there. Santa Fe has an interesting arts community, not large, but at least there are some good artists around. There are also several good galleries. I'm sure I could talk to the person who runs the gallery where I exhibit and get him to show your work as well."

I sat there dumbfounded, unable to speak. I had never considered a possibility like this. He went on. "This is a big decision, and I know it's a difficult one. Why don't you think about it. I'm here until the end of the week. That gives you several days to think it over. You can let me know what you want to do before I leave. Or, if you can't make a decision that quickly, go home and give it some serious thought. If you decide you want to come to Santa Fe, give me a call, and I'll do whatever I can to help you get settled."

I thanked him for everything, and for the offer, and walked out in a complete daze. My mind was racing, and I felt light-headed. I didn't know what to think or how to feel. I went back to my apartment and cried. It seemed so unfair to be forced into this dilemma, but Don was right. If I wanted to be an artist I couldn't continue as I had in the past.

I didn't mind the thought of leaving Mel, but what about the kids? Could I face the fact that they probably wouldn't want to leave their father and move out with me. I was almost certain that they would choose to stay with Mel. After the first divorce I learned the hard way where Gary wanted to be, and I was almost certain that Marc would follow the lead of his older brother.

I would have to make the choice to leave my children, and I didn't know if I could stand to live without them. I loved them dearly, but Mel had convinced them I was a little crazy, and that my passion for art was silly. When the time came to explain to them that I was moving to Santa Fe to pursue my career as an artist, I was certain they would side with their father and hate me even more than they already did.

Although it was painful to even think about life without my kids, it didn't take me long to decide what I had to do. I couldn't give up art. I just couldn't do it. I would do my best to explain this to my children and hope that somehow they would understand. But I didn't hold much hope. Deep in my heart I knew that my chances of making them understand were negligible.

Of course, I was right. I returned home at the end of the week, after Don left. The reception was not positive to say the least. All three of them were set on making me suffer for my absence as much as possible. Christmas was less than a week away, and so I tried to make the best of it. I got expensive gifts for both of the kids, and I tried to establish a nice holiday atmosphere around the house. Nothing worked, even though the kids loved their gifts.

After the first of the year, on an evening when Mel made several negative comments about my art, I decided that now was the time to tell him I was leaving. After dinner the kids went up to their rooms, and I finished washing the dishes. Mel came into the kitchen to get something out of the refrigerator. I decided this was the time.

"I have something to tell you. I've decided to move to Santa Fe to continue my art career. You have one of two choices. You can ask for a divorce, or we can stay married. If we stay married, you will have to accept a long-distance relationship. Or, you could find a teaching job in, or near, Santa Fe. Maybe, it's your turn to follow me."

He didn't even have to think about it. He said immediately that if I left he wanted a divorce, and he would do everything he could to keep me from seeing the kids. I told him that the kids were old enough to make their own decisions about who to live with and how much to visit the other person.

"With you running off for the last several months, and now leaving again," he blurted out, "we will see what a judge says." He then pushed me up against the kitchen counter, and grabbed my shoulders. "You are an absolutely pathetic excuse for a mother and a wife. You don't deserve to see, or have anything to do with your two children."

I came back immediately, "And you're so much better with all the women and teenage girls you've seduced."

All of a sudden a fist came out the air and landed a blow on the side of my face. I felt my legs go out from under me, and before I knew it I was on the floor. I may have blacked out at this point, I'm not sure, but when I looked down I could see blood streaming onto the floor. I couldn't get up. The pain in my face was intense, and I could feel a throbbing sensation in my jaw.

I then tried getting to my feet, but as I rose I felt a kick in my back that sent a shock wave through my entire body. I rolled over on the floor and tried to slide away from him, but I couldn't escape. He kicked me again, this time in the stomach. I gasped for air and began to choke. Blood was everywhere, but all I could do was lie there and try to breath. Finally, after several minutes standing over me, breathing heavily, he walked out of the room and out of the house.

After the pain subsided a little I was able to get to my feet. I limped into the bathroom, washed the blood from my face, and then headed straight to the bedroom to pack my bags. I knew I had to leave quickly, or things could get even worse. If I was still in the house when he returned, I was certain that he would become even more violent.

I realized that I would have to leave without talking to the kids, which made me sick just to think about it, but in some ways I thought it was better that way. They were completely on Mel's side, and the recriminations would have been more than I could stomach. I would try to call them in a couple of days after their initial anger subsided, and after they got used to the idea of my not living there any more. Maybe, I could find a way to communicate to them that I had to do this, and that I loved them dearly. I left as soon as my bags were packed and never went back.

Chapter 17

Philosophical Reflections

At this point it was well after six in the evening, and it was time for dinner. Emma agreed that we were overdue for a break. She commented that she couldn't believe she was telling me so much about her life. "I hope this sordid tale isn't too much for you," she said.

I assured her that nothing could be further from the truth, and that I wanted to hear more. "You've been through so much in your life. I just feel bad, really bad, that you had to go through all that. I had no idea that you had been physically abused by your husband. I just can't imagine what that was like. And to have your kids react the way they did. I thought I had it rough raising my daughter."

I shook my head in utter disbelief. "I've talked to a lot of artists over the years, and I must say that I've never heard of anything like this." Then I hesitated for a moment and thought about what I just said. "I wonder though, how many other women artists have gone through similar experiences, and we just don't hear about them? How many artists just like you are out there, stuck in the American heartland, unable to find anyone willing to hear their story? And how many women tried to become an artist, but eventually gave up under the obligations imposed by their family?"

She looked directly at me and said, "I think there are more out there than you can ever imagine. I was just lucky enough to be discovered by a big-time gallery owner."

I laughed. "Maybe I need to make a trip to the heartland and start visiting galleries out there."

She chuckled. "Yes, you would probably discover a number of artists, and at least some would show potential. But you would have to wade through a lot of terrible paintings, let me assure you. You see, the problem is that most of the people out in the Midwest and the West haven't had the opportunity of seeing good art on a regular basis, or interacting with dedicated and serious artists."

She stopped a minute and gathered her thoughts. "I'm sure that there are people, loyal to the heartland, who would disagree, who would point out that you can find a number of good museums that have large numbers of masterpieces, both from contemporary artists and historical figures. There are also good universities with art programs. However, I would reply that those museums and art programs simply aren't enough."

"I think I see what you mean," I said. "I must admit that I'm rarely tempted to leave New York and visit some museum in the middle of the country. There just isn't enough out there to make it worth the effort."

"Exactly," she said. "Although, theoretically, you can find good art instruction, and also see enough good art to get the background and training you need, the reality is that it's very hard for the aspiring artist to pass that illusory threshold necessary to become an artist on an internationally significant level. There simply isn't enough concentrated activity, like what you find in New York, or in European cities. Most artists out there, even the ones in some of the larger metropolitan areas, just haven't been able to get the kind of exposure and instruction that they so desperately need. They aren't connected to the frenzied, cutting edge art movements that happen on a regular basis in the cultural capitols of the world."

She laughed. "By the time we in the heartland were hearing of a new art movement in New York it was already yesterday's news to the artists here in the city. I was slightly luckier than most, but you must remember that I really wasn't able to do my best work until I made it to the East Coast, and was able to live here in Manhattan. Living in this wonderful city allowed me to immerse myself in an active and dynamic cultural scene. Here, I could go to galleries, meet other artists, and see what they were doing."

She paused to gather her thoughts and sip her glass of wine. "You also should know that in my senior years, although I'm by no means wealthy, I have been able to save just enough money to embark on a number of trips to Europe. For quite awhile I tried to make the trip to Europe once a year. I visited Paris, London, Berlin, Vienna, Florence, Venice, and a dozen other spots on that amazing continent, and I actually lived in Paris for about five months one year."

"Oh really," I replied. "I didn't know you spent that much time in Europe. I must say that will sound impressive to my collectors."

"Well" she said, "I can't begin to express to you how important, how enriching, that time in Europe was. I really think that my exposure to a wide range of significant art, both here on the East Coast and in Europe, has been the single most important factor allowing me to finally develop my style and my technique to its current level."

"I can't agree with you more," I replied. "One of the things that bothers me about a lot of the young artists I come in contact with here in New York is their lack of exposure to the art of Europe. Some simply don't understand how important that can be."

"You're so right," she replied with rising animation. "All those artists out there in the heartland, living in what I must describe as the cultural desert of America, haven't had the same opportunity as even those New York artists who haven't spent time in Europe. Sure, maybe there is an oasis here and there out in that desert, but even an oasis has a limited supply of water, and is very different from a lake. New York is a lake, the cities of Europe are lakes. Cities in the heartland of America are simply small, and in some cases, very small ponds.

She pointed to my shelves of books on one side of my living room. "I see in your bookcase several volumes of Henry James' writings. He addressed this very problem more than one hundred years ago. The only difference is that, in his time, the entire United States was a cultural backwater, not just the heartland, as it is for us today. Most of his novels and stories concern Americans traveling to Europe and encountering sophisticated culture for the first time. Many of his tales revolve around how the cultural depth of Europe changed these naive Americans. I would argue that James felt that one couldn't become an artist of any depth without leaving America and spending a protracted period in Europe."

"Your point is very interesting," I said. "You're making me want to go back and read some of his novels again."

"He's one of my favorite authors," she said, "and from the record of his time I think he was right. Just look at the most representative artists and literary figures of his era. He himself spent a good portion of his youth and most of his adult life in Europe. John Singer Sargent was actually born in Italy, grew up in Europe, and only made his first visit to the United States in early adulthood. Just think about it, he had never seen his own country until he was an adult.

James McNeil Whistler spent a good portion of his youth in Russia and England, and then, after being thrown out of West Point, returned to Europe and never again visited the United States. Edith Wharton also spent a large portion of her youth in Europe. She visited the continent for at least four months a year during the late 1880s and 1890s, and after her marriage ended, chose to live in France for the rest of her life. Even Thomas Eakins, that quintessential American realist, spent three years studying art in Paris before beginning his illustrious career in Philadelphia."

"I never thought about that," I said. "Yes, you're right. Almost all American artists of the late nineteenth century spent a number of years in Europe."

"It didn't stop with that generation," she continued. "The generation of American artists after James were also deeply influenced by their experience of Europe. In the early decades of the twentieth century, F. Scott Fitzgerald, Ernest Hemingway, Gertrude Stein, and Aaron Copland, to name only a few, all spent a number of years living in Europe. In fact, can we even imagine any of these artists' contribution to art and literature and music without thinking of their time in Europe?"

What Emma pointed out in this discussion was a revelation for me. Of course, I knew all these artists, but I had never thought about their experience, and the development of their style, from quite this angle. As I contemplated what she had a just said, I realized that this phenomenon was probably unprecedented in the history of art. Has any other country sent most of their major artists so far away to develop their "national" style? One could even raise the idea, at least in the case of James, Whistler, and Sargent, who each spent most of their lives outside of America, that they really aren't American artists. Yet, if you take them out of that era's ranks of American cultural figures, the list of those who could reasonably be classified as significant contributors to this country's culture shrinks significantly.

After I recovered my senses, I suggested that we make dinner at my apartment. She readily agreed, and we spent the next hour putting together a light meal. After we sat down to eat she continued her story.

As I drove to Santa Fe on that fateful night, over the long stretches of flat emptiness that one encounters in the eastern portion of New Mexico, where you can drive for miles and not even see another car, I assessed my situation. I had no money to speak of, no friends to call upon, no job, and my children probably wouldn't speak to me. I wondered if I could ever repair the damage with my children. With Mel, so good at convincing them of anything he wanted them to believe, I knew I was up against both their young emotions and his powers of persuasion.

I asked myself over and over again if pursuing the life of an artist was really worth it. Who knew if I had anything to offer that was truly original, or meant anything in a world I knew was crowded with mediocre artists. Creativity is a powerful stimulant. Was that stimulant, that I felt every time I picked up a brush, making it easy to deceive myself, to make me think that I had to do this. Was my need to create art simply a need to boost my ego?

I kept thinking of a quote that Don had used in one of his lectures at Texas Tech. He was introducing an experimental exercise that he wanted his students to try. He wanted them to draw a picture of a table with a large vase filled with flowers, and he wanted the students to do it without using an eraser. He explained that the idea behind the exercise was to help them learn that in some cases the best art comes out of mistakes, and finding ways to work with, or against, those mistakes.

The trick was to realize that a particular mistake could be something unique, and then figure out how to use your mistake to your advantage and develop the drawing from there. In order to help the students understand what was behind this exercise he quoted John W. Gardner, an official in President Lyndon Johnson's administration. Don said that he had heard this man give a lecture a couple of years earlier at the University of New Mexico, and had been especially impressed with one statement. Gardner had said that, "Life is the art of drawing without an eraser."

As I drove across New Mexico in the middle of the night I thought about this quote and knew that I couldn't go back. Maybe I was making a mistake, but life doesn't allow you to erase your mistakes and try again. You must simply work around, or use your mistakes, and move on with your life.

I realized, as I drove across the barren prairie on that lonely road, that being an artist wasn't something you necessarily chose to do. It was almost as if art chose you and forced you to live the life of an artist, the life of an outcast, not understood by the majority of humanity. I realized then, in the middle of that bleak night, that to be an artist was to be essentially estranged from most "normal" people. Many people might like art, or think they like it, but very few - even some people who think they're artists - understand what it really means to live the life of an artist, to be forced to isolate oneself and to pursue your singular vision.

That wasn't the only revelation of that horrible night. I also realized that it didn't matter if I was a "great" artist, or if I had anything really original to contribute. That assessment would be left to museum curators, art historians, and art critics, sometime in the distant future. I remembered that Van Gogh never sold a painting while he was alive. Did he think of himself as a success, or a failure? And does it really matter now? We can't possibly know what people a hundred years from now will think about the art we produce in our own time. Their values may not be our values, and what they find great may seem very strange to us.

Would Winslow Homer, or Thomas Eakins, appreciate, or even understand, abstract art, produced no more than fifty years after their passing? Or would Jacque Louis David, probably the greatest painter of the late eighteenth century, have understood Impressionism, which burst upon the art world no more than half a century after his death?

Whether I was an original artist or not didn't change the fact that I was compelled to create, to live the life of an artist, and to accept the ramifications of that lonely course. As I thought about all this, I remembered another quote by Henry James. "It is art that makes life, makes interest, makes importance, and I know of no substitute whatsoever for the force and beauty of its process."

Chapter 18

The Early Years in Santa Fe

When I arrived in Santa Fe I knew exactly what I had to do. Within just a couple of days I found a job as a waitress at a seedy truck stop restaurant on the edge of town. I think the woman who ran the restaurant hired me out of sheer pity once she saw the bruised and swollen face from Mel's brutal punch. The first thing she said when I walked in was, "I'll bet a man did that to you honey, am I right?" I confirmed her suspicions, and she hired me five minutes later. I then found a small efficiency apartment in a rundown complex behind a shopping center. The neighborhood wasn't the best, but I was in no position to be picky.

After I was settled in, and my face looked better, I was ready to call Don. When I got him on the phone I could tell he was surprised to hear my voice, but he was even more surprised to hear that I was in Santa Fe. I told him I had taken his advice and was ready to get back to work. He was excited to hear that I had "made the plunge," as he put it. Of course, he asked about what the situation was with my husband and kids. I told him the whole story, and he expressed regret that things had gone so badly, but he suggested that it was inevitable. "Your husband just doesn't understand what it means to be an artist, and how important your work is to you." He paused and then added, "Some people just can't understand the creative process."

After a little more conversation about where I was living, and the job I had taken, he invited me to his studio. "Come any day this week. Classes don't start at the university until the week after next, so I'm in my studio painting every afternoon."

I wanted to go see him the very next day, but I didn't want to seem too enthusiastic. I didn't want to make him think I was like an adoring, awestruck undergraduate. So I waited three days before I knocked on his door late one afternoon.

His studio was in an old office building in the downtown section of the city. The first floor of the building consisted of a couple of small stores with large display windows. The building looked like it had probably been built around the turn of the century and was a little worn and rundown. To the side of one of the stores was a narrow door that opened into a hallway. A rickety staircase led up to a second floor landing. This landing provided access to two doors. The one on the left led directly into his studio space. When I rang the doorbell I heard a distant shout that the door was open and to come in.

When I opened the door I immediately realized that his studio spanned the entire length of the building, with windows on three sides of the large open space. The ceiling was very high, which made the room seem even larger. There were paintings stacked everywhere. Paint cans, tubes of paint, brushes, dirty rags, and various other items one would expect to find in an artist's studio, littered the floor everywhere. Two easels were placed haphazardly in the middle of the room, and there was an old couch in bad need of upholstering, with a chair to the side, in one corner. Once I moved a few paces into the room, I could see that there was a small kitchen space, with a sink, a couple of cabinets, and an old refrigerator, behind a room divider.

He was standing at the sink busily washing several brushes. When he looked up, and saw me standing just a few feet inside the doorway, he waved me in and said, "So there you are. I was wondering when you might stop by. It's so good to see you. Please, come in. I'm just rinsing a couple of brushes. It won't take me a minute. Please look around and make yourself at home."

I walked over and nonchalantly dropped my purse on the couch, then took a second look around. "Nice space," I began. "You have a very open and spacious studio. Good light, lots of windows, and it looks like you have plenty of room."

"It's adequate," he replied. "I must admit that I've grown rather fond of this space." He walked into the middle of the room and thrust his hands into his pockets like a proud homeowner surveying his estate. "Yes, it's worked very well for what I need," he said with obvious pride.

He then ushered me over to a corner with several stacks of paintings leaning against the wall. "This is my most recent work," he began. "I've been fussing with these paintings since I got back from Lubbock."

He then spread out several of the paintings along the wall so I could look at each one. This was my first chance to see a large selection of his work. In his university-provided studio in Lubbock, really just an oversized office in one of the campus buildings, there were very few of his paintings available to see, and most of what he did bring with him was small.

Often, the studios provided by universities for visiting artists-in-residence are extremely cramped and inadequate. Don had explained that he worked better in his own studio, where he had everything he needed. He told his class that when he took these visiting professorships it was very hard to work, and so he saw these periods as an opportunity to take a break, teach, gain inspiration from his contact with student artists, and wait for the end of the semester to get back to his studio and get back to work. So I was largely unfamiliar with most of his art until this visit.

As I scanned the canvases he was pulling out for my inspection, I must say that I had an uneasy feeling as I viewed these paintings. Some of them seemed somewhat original, but there were other pieces that seemed overly fussy, even poorly executed. I still had so much to learn about art at this point in my life, but I already knew enough to know that he was clearly trying to follow in the footsteps of Georgia O'Keefe.

I would later learn that Don wasn't the only artist trying to imitate O'Keefe. At that time, in the late sixties, O'Keefe was still living out her declining years just up the road in Taos, New Mexico, and was already a legend. Several artists in Santa Fe, including Don, were imitating many of her stylistic characteristics in their own work.

I remember having just this slight tinge of a feeling that maybe I had made a mistake, that maybe Don wasn't the superstar artist I had thought from listening to his lectures in Lubbock. He had sounded so impressive then. When he worked with me individually, his advice seemed so perceptive. Yet, now that I was seeing a selection of his large paintings, I felt that somehow they just didn't live up to what I had expected to see. They weren't bad, but somehow they just didn't quite seem to be totally up to the level of what I had anticipated. But I quickly buried these troubling thoughts. I needed so much to believe that he was going to help me develop into a good artist, and he seemed so convincing when he talked about art.

As he explained what he was doing with each painting, he worked his magic again. As I listened to him elaborate on the various features of each of his creations, the ideas that had inspired each work of art, and how he had worked out a unique process of applying paint to the canvas, I began to think that my judgement had been too hasty. I wrote off my initial reaction to my lack of knowledge.

I also told myself that I had been too quick to judge him in a negative way simply because he had been influenced by O'Keefe. What did I expect I now reasoned. Every artist must have influences, and if he chose to be influenced by O'Keefe, well, why not. She was a well known artist, and was famous for her modernist style. On top of that, her desert scenes certainly seemed appropriate for artists working in New Mexico.

He then led me over to a large painting he had just started on the easel in the middle of the room. As we looked at the canvas, and he explained each of the elements of what he was trying to accomplish, he put his hand on the small of my back. It felt like an electric charge going through my body. I thought my knees were going to buckle, and it took every ounce of energy that I could summon to focus my concentration on what he was saying.

Then, all of a sudden, he stopped talking. I could feel him turn his head and look at me. I kept my eyes on the canvas, afraid to glance in his direction. The next thing I knew he was kissing me. Before I could even think of what was happening we were on the floor. He was pulling the light summer dress I was wearing off over my head, and I was fumbling with his belt buckle. Soon he was pushing me down on the floor and he was on top of me.

Looking back over all these years, I still think of where I was at that point. The pain I had just gone through, ending my marriage, leaving my children, and setting out to be an artist. Don seemed like a savior. He seemed like the one person willing to help me, to give me insight into the mysterious world of art and creativity. And I was attracted to him, I have no doubt about that. He was clever, knowledgeable, and had a touch of charisma. It was clear that his students loved him, and I felt fortunate that he had chosen me to award this special attention.

Over the next several months we sought out every opportunity to be together. Many evenings, as soon as I got off work, I stopped by my apartment, cleaned up quickly, and then headed straight for his studio. He would show me his latest paintings, we would talk, and more often than not wind up making love, usually on his old couch, or on the floor. A couple of times I had a sore back from rambunctious sessions on that hard and very unforgiving floor.

I worked on my paintings early in the morning before I went to work, or late at night after getting home from Don's studio. I had to make due with very limited space, so I set up an easel in one corner of my apartment. It was certainly not ideal, and it meant that the place was always a mess, with cans and tubes and brushes all over the kitchen table. I even sometimes used my bed to store supples, but I had very little choice at this point.

A few months later Don told me that a space had become available across the hall in his building. He suggested that I rent it and make it my studio. It wasn't really meant to be an apartment, but I couldn't afford to keep both. So I decided to rent the studio, give up my apartment, and live, as well as work, in the studio. It didn't even have a kitchen, just a sink and a small refrigerator, but I made it work.

During these early months with Don, I called the kids every week, sometimes more than once a week, but they refused to talk to me. Mel usually answered the phone and told me that they weren't interested in having anything to do with me, and that my efforts to call them were useless. I asked him to please tell them that I just wanted to talk to them for a few minutes, but he insisted that they didn't want to come to the phone. I didn't believe him, but what could I do.

Chapter 19

Early Attempts at Developing a Style

About a year after I moved to Santa Fe the divorce papers arrived in the mail, officially ending my marriage to Mel. This milestone worked in an odd way to free me to work more independently. I felt that I could close the book on my old life and pursue a direction that was much more centered on art. As my new existence took shape I was really inspired to put those hours in at the easel. Soon, I began to produce a number of paintings in a style very similar to Don's.

He had developed an approach that utilized and depicted scenes of the New Mexico desert. A typical painting by Don featured a low horizon line about a third of the way up from the bottom of the canvas. Below the horizon line he would brush in a hazy desert sand look, usually consisting of beige and brownish shades. Above the horizon line he painted a vast blue field that could be read as a clear sky. Often, he would add scratched, jagged lines penciled on this surface, which might represent bushes, or dried vegetation to the viewer.

Since he watered down his paint quite a bit, his colors were very bright and translucent. He almost never used dark colors. In fact, so much of the painting was taken up by the blue sky that it made his work seem almost abstract and very minimal. His paintings were practically nothing more than a large beige square on the bottom of the canvas and a large blue rectangle on the top. Of course, since minimalist art was very much in vogue at that time, his work seemed very up-to-date.

For those who couldn't quite stomach modern art, like Abstract Expressionism, with its chaotic and haphazard brushstrokes, too messy and confusing, these paintings were perfect. Don's work was easy on the eye, and for those viewers who needed art to represent something concrete, his paintings could easily be interpreted as desert landscape scenes. Yet, they also seemed to exude a clean, modern look. This made them especially attractive to collectors who wanted to show how knowledgeable and up-to-date they were about abstraction and modernism, and yet weren't comfortable with what they thought of as weird and ugly contemporary art.

Many collectors who came into the gallery that displayed Don's art recoiled from any abstract painting that was the least bit aggressive, or featured dark or dissonant colors. After all, you didn't want some radical modernist monstrosity in your house. What would your friends think? But Don's work didn't suffer from any of these characteristics. Of course, since everyone seemingly liked light blue and beige, these paintings fit with the decor of collector's homes perfectly.

Which reminds me of how good he was at gallery openings. He was great at playing the role of the slightly bohemian, but very friendly, artist. The various collectors who came to these openings were intrigued by his personality. They would gather around Don, and listen to him elaborate on all the intricacies of his paintings. I often stood to the side and listened with fascination as he waxed on eloquently.

Being a good student, I was soon producing paintings in a very similar style to Don's. I used translucent, watered down paint in order to create the effect of a bright and open desert sky, but avoided the horizon line he always used. In order to make sure that my work didn't look too much like his, I painted large desert flowers, something he never did.

That approach seemed like a good way to avoid the typical Santa Fe painter's canvas of two large rectangles of color hinting at a landscape. But I must admit that my flower idea wasn't that unique either. There were several artists working then who were doing various versions of desert flowers as well. I knew I was following Don's lead for the most part, and I knew that many people in the arts community around Santa Fe saw me as nothing more than Don's protege. It was a simple matter that, at this point, I didn't know how to avoid that impression.

Within a short time, a few cracks began to develop in my life as a new artist under Don's tutelage. The first noticeable change was that Don stopped making suggestions about how I could improve my paintings. In fact, after just a few months, he rarely said anything, good or bad, about my work. In a short time it became blindingly obvious that he was much more interested in having sex with me than he was in helping me with my paintings. But I put up with it since, at this point in my evolution as an artist, I felt a desperate need for guidance. I clung to him for a lot longer than I should have.

I think that one reason he stopped helping me with my paintings was that he started seeing me as potential competition. The first thing that made me aware of his increasing concern was a couple of unexpected acknowledgments of the quality of my work. A little more than a year after I arrived in Santa Fe the owner of a prominent gallery in New York came to town. He had heard of Don's work from another Santa Fe artist who had moved to New York, and while he was in town, he wanted to see Don's paintings. After I heard about this visitor coming to town, I asked Don if I could go with him when he met this gallery owner. After introductions, Don walked him around the gallery showing him his work. The man was very polite, but didn't seem that enthusiastic about Don's paintings.

After awhile he approached me and asked if I was an artist. When I confirmed that I was, he asked to see my paintings. I shyly pointed to several of my canvases that were then on display in the gallery. I was so embarrassed. After seeing his response to Don's work, I was sure he would think that my paintings were terrible. But he really liked them. I didn't know what to say. He walked to each one, asked a few questions, and then moved on to the next one. In front of several of my canvases he commented that my work was very good. A little later, when Don was talking to another person on the other side of the room, the man pulled me over to the side and asked if I had ever thought of moving to New York.

"No," I said. "To be honest with you I haven't considered that."

"Well," he replied, "you should." He paused and looked directly at me with what seemed to me a very intense and disconcerting stare. "I really think that working in New York, having contact with the art world there, would be a very good experience for you. Your work shows real potential. I don't think you're completely ready for an exhibit in New York yet. You need more exposure to the latest trends, and to some of the better art being produced right now."

He looked over at Don to make sure he wasn't listening to our conversation. "If you would be willing to spend a little time getting to know what is current, possibly develop a better understanding of what the best work being produced is all about, I think you're art would evolve and mature in a very positive direction. If you would like to come to New York let me know."

He reached into a pocket of his suit jacket and pulled out a small card, which he held casually between two fingers, waving it in the air in front of me. "Here's my card. I'll be more than happy to help you settle in New York, and I'll do everything I can to get you off to a good start."

I was almost speechless. I choked out a thank you.

He replied immediately, "I'm very serious about this. I think you could do well in my gallery."

"What about Don's work?" I asked.

He hesitated. "I appreciate his willingness to take the time to show me his work. It's very..." he hesitated again. I could tell he was trying to find a diplomatic response. "His work is very characteristic of New Mexico artists. There's a certain," another hesitation, "a certain spontaneity in it. But I'm afraid his paintings wouldn't work in my gallery."

I was totally shocked by this encounter, first because the owner of a prominent gallery in New York had taken an interest in my art, but also because he had rejected Don's work, and implied that he was, at best, a good regional artist. From then on I began seriously questioning the value of Don's art.

When we got back to his studio that day I could tell that Don was mad. "What a jerk," he railed, as he poured himself a scotch. "Who does he think he is," he continued. "He didn't even take the time to really study my paintings. He wasn't even willing to visit my studio. I don't even know why I bothered to offer him the opportunity. It was clear that he wasn't serious about understanding the range of my work."

I tried my best to sound sympathetic, but I don't know how convincing I was. Then everything blew up. A couple of days later, one of his artist friends told him that he had heard through the rumor mill that a New York gallery owner was interested in my work. As soon as he heard this he headed straight to my studio. I was working on a canvas when the door flung open and he marched into the room. "What did that New York snob say to you?" Don yelled, clearly heated.

I tried to play the whole conversation down, and make it sound like it wasn't anything important. "He just said that he liked a few of my paintings. He said that I had some potential to do good work. He also suggested that I really wasn't up to par now, but that I might improve my work if I came to New York."

"What a load of crap," Don fumed. "What audacity that man has. To suggest that the only good art is art created by painters in New York is about as snobbish as it gets. I'm sure he thinks that you have to be in his little 'in crowd' in Soho to be worth anything at all. What an arrogant bastard."

He paused a minute, shaking his head from side to side and pacing the floor of my studio. Then he began again. "I'll bet that the real reason he was interested in your paintings is because you are a woman. He probably thought that if he complemented you on your work he could get between your legs. What a jerk."

I wanted to remind him that the first time I visited his studio he had also shown a strong interest in getting between my legs, but I didn't want to make him madder than he already was. And his theory was plausible. Who knows what this gallery owner's motivation was. I certainly wasn't certain, at this stage in my career, that my art was good enough to attract the attention of a New York gallery owner, but down deep inside I knew that Don was just jealous.

Over the next several months this whole episode made me begin to think that maybe you did need to be in New York in order to develop a truly original style. I thought about the history of painting and realized that most great artists through the centuries were usually located in one of the major art centers of that time: in Florence, Rome, or Venice during the Renaissance, or Paris and Vienna during the nineteenth century. Maybe. it was essential to rub shoulders with other important artists in order to make a lasting contribution to art.

Think of the story of Van Gogh, who only developed his signature Impressionist style after arriving in Paris and seeing the work of other Impressionists, or Picasso, who truly was one of the most gifted artists of any age. Would he have pioneered the innovations of Cubism if he had stayed in provincial Spain? How much did his exposure to the hothouse environment of Paris contribute to his ability to bring about one of the greatest breakthroughs in the art of the twentieth century?

As I said earlier, my initial inspiration came from seeing the work of the Abstract Expressionists, and since that first glimpse I had learned that almost all the major figures of that movement socialized together at a single bar in lower Manhattan, the Cedar Tavern. Maybe I needed to find out where artists were hanging out now, and see if contact with a few of the most up-to-date styles might improve my work.

I floated these ideas by Don in as diplomatic a fashion as I could. In fact, we had several discussions about it over the four or five months after the visit from the New York dealer, and Don did listen to what I had to say. I could tell that he had thought about the possibility of going to New York even before this recent episode. But in the end he rejected the idea.

"Everyone thinks they have to go to New York. I just don't buy it. Santa Fe has an interesting and vibrant arts community, and there are some really good artists here. Don't forget," he said. "This is where Georgia O'Keefe chose to live." I wanted to remind him that O'Keefe had spent a good number of years in New York before coming to New Mexico, but I thought better of it. I could see that he was convinced that living in New York wasn't necessary.

Of course, at the time, I thought he might be right. After all, his reasoning did make some sense. He was well known among New Mexico artists, and he was a professor of art at the University of New Mexico. I knew that all that would be hard to give up on the slight chance of making it in New York.

To add to Don's argument I remembered the fact that both of us weren't exactly young artists anymore. It might be one thing to run off to New York when you're 23 or 24. But at our age it might be too late to really get anything out of the experience.

I thought that fact especially applied to Don. He seemed so set in what he was doing that I couldn't imagine him changing. I thought that I might change, since I wasn't totally happy with what I was creating, and I saw myself then as in the early stages of developing a unique style. But Don seemed so pleased with what he was doing that I imagined he would probably sit in a New York studio and continue to create paintings of the New Mexico desert.

Yet, in retrospect, I think the main reason he didn't want to go to New York was that he was afraid that he might not be good enough. The rejection by the New York dealer certainly didn't build his confidence. Ultimately, I think it came down to the simple fact that he was a big fish in a little pond in Santa Fe, and he was afraid that he would be eaten by the bigger fish in New York.

It wasn't as if I couldn't identify with his dilemma. As much as the idea of going to New York excited me, I also wondered what would happen if I went and failed. Thousands of aspiring artists get off the bus in the city every year, and very few find even minimal success. I also wondered what it would be like to live in New York. At this point, I had never been to the city, and it scared me to think about simply pulling up stakes, leaving the only region I had ever lived in, and moving to such a large city. Even though I really wanted to take up the invitation of the New York dealer, I remained in Santa Fe for the time being, trying to figure out what to do.

Chapter 20

My Art Takes a New Direction

My work changed drastically after the encounter with the New York dealer. I no longer saw Don as a mentor, and as I explained, I began to feel that his art was limited and regional. I had been itching to try some new ideas for some time before, now I felt liberated to break away from what he was doing.

Rather than continue to produce tepid paintings of the New Mexico desert and sky, like Don, I went back to my original inspiration, the work of the Abstract Expressionists, especially the work of Joan Mitchell and Grace Hartigan. I was especially enamored with Mitchell's work. Her paintings, with slashing, violent brushstrokes exploding across the canvas, seemed so alive and vibrant and aggressive. At this point, I too wanted to be aggressive. I was so sick and tired of the vacuous paintings that most of the Santa Fe artists I knew were painting.

One of the first paintings I attempted after this change of style was a brooding work, with slashing strokes of blood-red piercing through a dark web of blue and black patches. I wasn't sure that the painting had any merit at all. I just felt that I had to follow my instincts and keep working on it. One afternoon, as I was adding some final touches to this painting, Don happened to walk by my studio space. When he saw what I was doing, he stopped dead in his tracks and studied the painting. I could tell he was surprised by my new direction and was trying to figure out what I was doing. I waited while he looked over the canvas, wondering if he thought it a total disaster, or if he thought it might have potential. After several minutes he finally said, "It looks like you're having fun," and then he walked out.

I was totally taken aback. "Having fun" was all he could come up with. The very fact that he had trouble understanding what I was doing, where I was going with this work, made me feel that I was finally beginning to do something that was truly original. I began to realize that the limitations of his vision, his restricted understanding of some contemporary works, was the very reason that he was limited as an artist. Developing into a great painter is so much more than the ability to draw or paint. Great art requires an extraordinary vision, a totally original perception of the world. I don't necessarily think I had found all the answers then, but I was onto something that had, at least, a degree of true originality.

The last straw in our relationship came when he was asked to curate a show of the most representative New Mexico artists on the contemporary scene. He selected works of almost all his friends, but left me out. When I realized that I wasn't included in the show, I confronted him, and we were soon locked in a heated argument. But he stuck tenaciously to his position and insisted that what I was doing didn't fit well with the other artists in the exhibit. When the show opened, and my work wasn't on view, many of his friends were surprised, and asked him about it, but he didn't care. He didn't like what I was doing, and that was the end of the discussion as far as he was concerned.

We had another disagreement when the New York dealer contacted me about six months after his original visit and asked if I could send several of my most recent paintings to Soho for an upcoming show in his gallery. When I agreed, Don saw it as a total betrayal.

After that dispute, I packed the paintings and sent them off. I hoped that this would lead to greater recognition, even if I wasn't based in the city, but the exhibit failed to lead to anything more. After the show was over, the gallery owner said that my work had been noticed by several collectors, and he wanted to do more for me. Then he repeated what he had said earlier. He wasn't willing to go to that effort unless I was in New York.

"You need to be where the action is, and let me tell you, it isn't in fly-over country." This dealer could be very obnoxious about art in the provinces, and it irritated me when he made these comments, but I had to admit that he was right. It's like trying to study advanced physics without going to a university. Maybe it can be done, but it certainly isn't easy.

Then, just around the time I was contemplating going to New York, after almost two long years of no contact with my children, the phone rang one day, and my oldest son Gary was on the other end of the line. He had decided that he wanted to see me. He wanted to have a chance to talk to me about things. I was absolutely ecstatic, and it took everything in my power just to keep from breaking down right there as I held the phone in my hand. He said he wanted to come visit in a couple of weeks. He asked if that was acceptable. I remember telling him that he never, ever had to ask that question. "I want to see you more than anything in the world. And you can come and visit anytime for as long as you want."

When he did finally come, I remember how terribly nervous I was. I could hardly eat for several days before he arrived. When he pulled his car into the driveway and got out of the car, I almost didn't recognize him. It was amazing how much he had changed in so short a time. The last time I had seen him he was just an awkward teenage boy of sixteen. Now he seemed so much more mature. After he got out of the car, and pulled his bags out of the trunk, he walked up the driveway and gave me a hug. I almost collapsed right there on the spot. I had to summon every ounce of strength in my power just to keep from bursting into tears.

At first, our interactions were cordial and slightly restrained. He held back, keeping the conversation general and trivial. I wanted desperately to reach out to him, to embrace him more fully. I wanted so much to walk up to him and give him hugs, but I took his cue and kept my distance.

On the evening he arrived, we went out for a nice dinner. I asked Don to join us, thinking that maybe having him as another person to talk to might make it easier for Gary to adjust to being around me again. Don wound up talking to Gary more than I did. They seemed to get along really well. They talked about a variety of things, everything from politics to sports. Since this was Gary's first visit to Santa Fe, Don offered to show him around town and introduce him to the local sites. I just sat and listened to their animated conversation most of the time.

Gary's visit also gave me a chance to catch up on what the family was doing and what I had missed over the last two years. Mel hadn't wasted any time moving on. Within a year he was already involved with another woman, a women who wasn't much older than Gary. They had met at the school where Mel taught. She was just out of college and in her first year of teaching. Of course, I could easily picture Mel making his move and sweeping her off her feet before she knew what hit her. They were married before the end of the school year.

The other big news was that Mel had fallen into financial trouble. Gary, of course, made all kinds of excuses for his dad. I could tell he was still totally under his father's sway. One thing was very clear. Without me around to slow down his spending on whatever caught his eye he had swiftly descended into debt. Right after he and his new bride got married they were forced to move to Shamrock, Texas, another little spot in the road near the Oklahoma border. There, Gary finished high school. Marc, now thirteen, was having trouble adjusting to his new school in Shamrock, but Gary felt that things would probably improve when he went back to school in the fall.

Gary was excited about his upcoming plans. He had been accepted at McMurry College, the same school his father and I had attended, and was looking forward to beginning. He planned to major in business.

"So you're following in the footsteps of your father," I began. "I have to say, back in the 50s, when you're father and I were there, it wasn't much of a college."

"What does that mean," he immediately snapped back. I realized I had made a mistake, and had opened my mouth before I thought how he would take it.

"Just because you didn't have a good experience there doesn't mean it's a bad school. You didn't even finish your degree. Dad says it's an excellent school, and I'll enjoy the experience there."

I realized I had to repair things quickly. I didn't want to alienate him before we had a chance to reconnect. "I'm sorry," I began, "I didn't mean that the way it sounded. I was just trying to say that the school was a lot smaller when I was there. I'm sure it's much better now. Your father's right. I'm sure you'll have a great college experience there."

I shifted the discussion and asked him what courses he planned to take his first year. Everything he mentioned was a business course. I encouraged him to give it some time before making a decision about a major, and to consider taking a few humanities courses, but I could tell that he really wasn't interested in hearing my advice. After listening to me make my recommendations he put me off by saying he would keep an open mind and changed the subject.

After that discussion, which took place on the second day of his visit, Gary's tone began to change subtly. I could feel his resentment and anger rising just under the surface of his cordial conversational interactions.

On the third day, as we sat in my studio and sipped iced tea, his rage finally boiled to the surface. I was telling him how much I enjoyed working as an artist in Santa Fe. I thought that I could somehow show him how much it meant to me to be an artist, and how meaningful the practice of art had been for me the last decade. I hoped that he might begin to understand why I felt compelled to leave two years earlier. But Gary didn't respond as I had expected.

"I guess that what you're saying is that this," waving his arms at the studio full of paintings, "was what made you, compelled you, to leave me, Dad, and Marc. Is it really so wonderful that you just couldn't wait to escape us? What is so terribly important about making a lot of paintings?"

He shook his head in disgust and let out a sarcastic laugh. "I guess it's a big ego trip being an artist," he continued. "It must be very cool to see your paintings in some fancy gallery. I guess it really makes you feel grand to have someone admire one of your paintings and tell you how

171

brilliant and creative you are." He paused deep in thought. I remained silent.

"I kind of get it. It's nice to be creative. You feel like you're saying something important. But when you were showing me your paintings yesterday I just kept thinking that how could this, these ridiculous paintings - that look like you hurled paint across the canvas - how could this be worth leaving your two children."

He let out a disgusted hiss. "Maybe it wasn't just the art. Don seems like a nice person. I understand that he's known as an important artist around here. In fact, I think - although I'm no expert on art - that I like his paintings more than yours. His desert scenes are kind of interesting. So maybe what attracted you to this kind of life was the chance to hang out with artists. I get it. The art scene is kind of cool, and being around important artists must be kind of exciting."

He walked around my studio looking at the paintings scattered around the room. Then he continued. "Life with Dad must have seemed kind of drab in comparison. Since he isn't creative, maybe he was boring to you. Maybe your two children were boring to you as well. We couldn't discuss art with you like your friends could. We aren't creative geniuses like all your artist friends are. But you have to understand what that did to us. I'm trying to at least connect with you and get to know you again, although I'm not sure why. But your other son - remember him - still doesn't want to have anything to do with you. I can't blame him. I wasn't totally sure that I wanted to come and see you either."

I was stunned and completely drained after listening to my son say these things. I sat there unable to speak, desperately trying to hold back the tears. I had known that he and his brother were angry with me. How could they not feel anger after what they had gone through. But I didn't realize just how virulent their anger had grown, or how distorted their picture of what happened had become.

Although I tried to hold back my emotions, soon the tears were rolling down my face. I could see, out of the corner of my eye, that Gary noticed. He just rolled his eyes and turned away in disgust. I wanted to address each of his points, and try to explain how understandable but wrong he was in his perceptions, but I realized that there was very little

I could do to change his perspective. There was just too much anger to overcome. I didn't feel like I could really tell him the total truth.

How could I tell him that the father he thought of so highly was a total liar, a con-artist, and had seduced several of his underage students, to say nothing of the numerous sexual encounters with other women. I kept telling myself that he's just eighteen years old. He's still so innocent.

I knew that if I tried to tell him about what I had been forced to go through from almost the beginning of my marriage he wouldn't believe me. I was sure that he would think that I was just trying to justify my actions. How could I tell him how his father had treated me, that there were times I was afraid of being beaten, or even worse? How could I say that the reason I had left without saying goodby that awful night, two years earlier, was that his father had punched and kicked me, and that I was afraid of what he might do to me if I was still there when he returned home that night?

Instead, I tried to talk about what it was like to be an artist, the drive, the fact that I had felt that I didn't really have a choice between being an artist and choosing not to pursue art. I tried to explain to him that if I had given up art, I felt then, and still feel now, that I would have died.

His response was totally without sympathy or any degree of understanding. "Aren't you being a little dramatic," he said, as he rolled his eyes noticeably. "Do you really expect me to think that your choice was between life and death. Come on!"

At this point I was desperate to show him that I really cared about him and his brother. I now tried a different approach. "It wasn't all my fault that I wasn't able to see you," I began. "I tried repeatedly to see you, and tried to work out arrangements to share custody, to work it out so that you and your brother could visit me on a regular basis. Your father wouldn't hear of it. I tried to get a judge to let me see you, but you know how persuasive your father can be. He convinced the judge that I had abandoned the family, and that was enough to convince the judge to rule against me."

I wiped the tears from my eyes. "I didn't give up even then," I continued. "I begged Mel repeatedly to let me see you and your brother, but he wouldn't let me. Surely, you can see that I never wanted to abandon the two of you. If your father had been more reasonable I could have continued to spend a lot of time with you, but he wouldn't budge. Surely you can agree that his actions were unfair, not only to me, but to the two of you."

Gary furrowed his brow and seemed somewhat disturbed by these remarks. I gathered that the fact that I had tried to work out an arrangement where I could visit him and his brother came as something of a surprise, and he was now trying to process this new information. I don't think he had considered this possibility. His father had convinced him that I had simply abandoned the family, but now my remarks had sewn some doubt.

He remained silent for several minutes, and I thought it best to let him think. Finally, he came up with a reply. I could tell that it was important to him to maintain the moral high ground. "It's nice to know that you made at least some effort to see us. But the fact remains that you are the one that left the family, and you didn't even say goodby to your two children."

I remained silent for several minutes, and then tentatively began a defense. "I'm so sorry that things turned out the way they did," I whispered. "It was a difficult time for me, and I tried to do the best I could. I may have made some choices that weren't the best, and I may have not handled everything as well as I should have, but I can only say that I tried to make the best of a bad situation, and I never stopped loving the two of you."

The next day he left. As he was loading the car with his bags, I begged him to return soon. I also asked him to convey to his brother my sincere interest in having him visit at any time. He was cordial but noncommittal, saying simply, "I'll convey the message, but don't count on hearing from him."

As he drove off I had a good long cry. I had so hoped that things would go better, and that Gary would realize how much I loved him. All I could do at this point was hold onto the hope that I had possibly given him a few things to ponder, things that he hadn't considered before his visit. Regrettably, my efforts were totally in vain. There were no future visits from either of my two sons, and it would be many years before I saw Gary again. Marc continued to hold a terrible grudge against me, and I never saw him again.

After Gary left, I resumed my life as an artist in Santa Fe, but with each passing day I felt less connected to what was happening on the local art scene. Not a day passed that I didn't think about the invitation to go to New York. I kept asking myself what was stopping me. The big city seemed so scary, so overwhelming in its immensity, but I increasingly came to feel that I had to face this challenge head on. I couldn't let fear overcome what I knew I needed to do. Finally, about a year after Gary's visit, during the hot summer of 1970, shortly after I had turned 40, I packed my bags and got on a bus headed for New York.

Chapter 21

My New York Experience

When I arrived in New York and walked out of the bus station, I couldn't believe what I was seeing. I thought I knew what big cities were like. I had lived in El Paso and Lubbock, and I had been to Chicago, but nothing prepared me for the density and flood of sensations brought about by the abundance of Manhattan. The sidewalks were clogged with people scurrying about, heading in all directions at once. It seemed like thousands of people were swarming around me, and I was caught in an insect-like maze of human activity.

I couldn't keep from looking up at the skyscrapers lifting up into a dazzling blue sky. I was overwhelmed by the number and height of these monstrosities. After a minute or two I realized that my standing on the sidewalk, with two bags in my hands, just staring at this startling world swirling around me, had created a roadblock, and that these busy New Yorkers were becoming annoyed as they worked their way around the nuisance I had become. They must have all thought that I was a typical country bumpkin, which is exactly what I was.

I began to walk, ambling along, moving much slower than these fast-walking and determined New Yorkers, not really knowing where I was going, carried along by the frenzied rush around me. I began to notice details of this urban conglomeration. There were people of every make, description, age, and ethnic origin. Garbage, in some places piles of it, and yellow taxi cabs, and storefronts filled with all sorts of merchandise, were everywhere, attacking my senses, and sending me into a state of confusion.

After several blocks I found myself in front of a small cafe with a long counter along one wall. I realized that I had to get my bearings and figure out what to do next. I couldn't just keep walking with no plan or purpose. I stepped in and found a seat at the counter. Nobody seemed to notice my entry, and the activity of the place seemed to continue unabated, oblivious to my presence. I waited several minutes, just looking around, trying to gain some relief for my overloaded brain.

Finally, a waiter came over to take my order. I asked for a ham sandwich and tea. "Iced or hot?" came the question from the busy woman. I was surprised by the question. I had never been asked such a question in the South. In Texas or New Mexico, during the summer, it was assumed that if you asked for tea surely you were asking for iced tea. I answered iced tea, and she scurried away. I immediately realized that this was a very strange place. I couldn't even order food at a restaurant in the same way as I had in the South.

After finishing my sandwich and iced tea, I headed out to look for a hotel. Wandering down the street for a couple of blocks, I saw a nice hotel and thought this would be a good place to initiate my experience of the city. I walked into the lobby and headed straight for the reception desk. I asked for a room, and as the man at the counter was filling out the paperwork, I realized that I hadn't asked the price of the room. Once he informed me, I was dumbfounded. I had never heard of a hotel renting rooms at this price. I stuttered.

His pen stopped and lifted from the form in front of him. "Is there a problem?"

"I'm sorry," I replied hesitantly, "I think I've changed my mind." I hurried out of the lobby as fast as I could.

I walked a couple of more blocks and tried another hotel. Again, the price seemed astronomical. At the third hotel I summoned the courage to ask the desk manager if there was somewhere in the area that was a little less expensive. He gave me a look like I was some homeless person off the street in bad need of a bath. He suggested a hotel several blocks away that would "fit my needs," as he put it.

I walked to the hotel he had suggested and could see immediately why it was cheaper. The lobby furniture, a faded rust color, looked like they had been purchased for a significant discount at a used furniture store. The floor looked like it had last been cleaned a year or two earlier. But the price was right, and I wound up staying in this dump for the next two weeks.

After dropping my bags and collapsing on the bed, I slept for at least the next ten hours. When I awoke the next morning I felt much better. I was ready to take on the city and the world. After pancakes, and this time - hot tea - at a nearby breakfast place, I was ready to call the gallery owner who had lured me to this strange city. After two calls, in which I was informed that he wasn't available, I finally succeeded in getting him on the phone late in the afternoon.

"Hi Emma," he began as soon as he picked up the receiver. "I hear that you've finally made it to the city. Welcome to New York." I could hear a voice in the background talking to him, though I couldn't make out what she was saying.

"Listen, Emma, I only have a minute. Things are just crazy around here. What can I do for you?" I thought he would help me find an apartment and maybe a studio, and that he would help me get started in the city, but it became apparent very quickly that I was expected to just figure all that out on my own. So I shifted to asking him about my art.

"Did you get the delivery of my paintings?" I asked.

"Yes, yes, they came in last week. We were glad to see them arrive. They're all here."

"So what's our next step?" I asked.

"Don't worry about a thing. We have a group show coming up very soon, and you are definitely on our list of artists. The opening reception is... wait," he yelled to an assistant asking when the reception was scheduled. I could hear a voice in the distance. "Right, the opening reception is scheduled for October 6th. Put that on your schedule. Don't miss it. I definitely want to see you there."

Another muffled voice in the background. "Listen Emma, I must go. It's been great talking with you. Again, welcome to New York." And then the line went dead.

I realized immediately that I was in a strange city, where I knew no one, and I was most certainly on my own.

After spending the rest of the day seriously contemplating purchasing a return bus ticket back to New Mexico, I wound up in a nearby bar. As I sat in this dark and slightly seedy establishment through most of the evening, I finally talked myself into staying and trying to make a go of it. I reasoned that, since I was already here, I had nothing to loose by giving it a shot. I kept saying to myself that eight million other people lived in this city. If they can do it, surely, I can as well. I'm also fairly certain that the large amounts of alcohol consumed that night helped fortify my resolution.

I realized that I had to start fresh, just as I had when I arrived in Santa Fe. I immediately began looking for a job. Since I had plenty of experience as a waitress, that was the path I pursued in New York. When I noticed that a twenty four hour diner had a help wanted sign in the window, I walked in and asked for the job.

A tired looking man in his fifties interviewed me. "What brings you to New York?" he asked.

"I'm an artist, I paint" I replied.

He laughed. "Everybody comes to New York as an artist, and everyone leaves New York as something else." Needless to say I didn't get the joke.

We were then interrupted by a patron. When he returned we continued our conversation. "I too came to New York with big dreams," he said. "Many years ago I came here to make it big writing novels. Now I run this dump."

He paused for a minute, looking me over. "Well, I don't want anyone to accuse me of not encouraging art. So, I guess you're hired. The only shift we have available is the night shift. Will working at night harm your inspired creativity," he joked.

"No, I think that will work well for me." And with that I had a job in the city.

Soon I was into my routine at the diner. I spent each night serving drunks who came in to get out of the cold and have a cup of coffee, their hands shaking with each sip. There were also a lot of prostitutes who stopped in, taking a break from the street. The beginning of my shift, the hours around midnight, were usually very busy. But around three or four in the morning business dropped off, and I usually spent those hours reading.

After I got off work at around seven, I usually spent the rest of the morning, and sometimes part of the afternoon, sleeping. Then I got up and had a light meal. I usually spent the remainder of the afternoon painting or visiting galleries. Occasionally, I would visit a museum. One of the main reasons I had come to New York was to learn about art, especially the art of the moment, and so I remained vigilant in my efforts to see as many exhibits as I could.

After I got a job my next task was to find a place to live. I couldn't wait to get out of that awful hotel. But I can't say that I moved up the social scale that much when I finally found an apartment. All that I could afford was a small studio in a rundown building, and when I say small I mean really small. The whole unit was smaller than most bedrooms in houses back in Texas and New Mexico.

It featured a bathroom that was so cramped that the sink and the toilet were practically in the shower. The "kitchen" was really a sink and a small refrigerator stuck in the corner behind the front door. The rest of the room consisted of a pull-out couch and a small table with a lamp on it. When you pulled the bed out, the mattress extended to within one inch of the opposite wall. In fact, when the bed was extended, I was forced to climb over it in order to get into the bathroom. The one window gave me a wonderful view of the solid brick wall of the neighboring building just six feet away.

Yet, it's amazing how adaptable we are as humans, and I quickly got used to it. I soon located a small grocery down the street, and other shops that I needed were within a couple of blocks one way or another. I actually got to a point that I liked this little room. It was cozy, and I actually figured out how to use it as a studio as well. If the bed was tucked away, I had just enough room for my easel and paint supplies.

Within a couple of weeks I was settled in enough to begin working on my art. As I produced paintings I had no storage, so I started hanging them on the walls flush against one another. When I needed more space, I began to hang them on top of the others. Soon, paintings were on every wall from floor to ceiling. Having all my paintings flush against each other like that made me begin to see things in these works that I hadn't noticed before, and it actually led to ideas that I incorporated into later paintings.

Finally, the big day arrived, and I made my way to the gallery for the opening reception of the group show that I had been told I would be one of the featured artists. When I entered the gallery, I could see that there were already thirty, or maybe thirty-five, people milling around, talking and sipping wine. No one noticed my entry, and I stood in the entrance, not quite knowing what I should do next.

The gallery consisted of a large warehouse-like space with several smaller rooms to one side. I looked around at the art. The first thing I noticed was the absence of paintings on display. Most of what I could see from this vantage point were sculptures of various shapes and sizes, and various installation pieces. The only paintings visible were a couple of severely minimalist creations on a far wall. These two paintings consisted of a white background with a single diagonal line, about an inch thick, from the upper left corner to the lower right corner of the canvas. For variety, the second canvas placed the line in a slightly different location and was in a different color.

My paintings were nowhere to be seen. I walked around the main gallery to see if I could find my paintings. I confirmed that they weren't in that space, so I began to explore the side rooms. Finally, I walked into the last small room at the back of the gallery, almost ready to give up hope. When I first entered, I was met by a large pile of dirt, with a television in an unpainted wooden box, placed on top of the pile. The video running on the television was a film of nude women writhing on the floor.

On the side wall was a sculpture that consisted of a block of concrete with three pieces of metal rebar sticking out of the concrete. It looked like some ancient fossilized insect from the Jurassic period. When I made my way around the pile of dirt with the television on it, there they were, two of my paintings. The first thought that came to mind, as I surveyed the location of my canvases, was how out of place they looked in this space, but at least a couple of my paintings were on display. I had started to think that the gallery had decided to delete my work from the show.

I made my way out to the main room and looked for Leo, the gallery owner. I finally spotted him on the other side of the room, surrounded by a group of people. Everyone was listening to him tell a story. It must have been very funny, based on the faces of the people in the group. I waited a few feet away, pretending to look at a pile of rocks that I was fairly certain was meant to be interpreted as a sculpture.

When I saw an opening, I made my move, and walked up and greeted the proud gallery owner with a chirpy, "Hi Leo. Great show!"

"Oh, hi Emma. So glad you could make it. So you like the show. I'm so pleased. Great to see you."

Before I could say anything else three people walked up to him, and immediately began praising the exhibit. I don't think they even noticed that I was standing there. Before long he was pulled away, and I stood there, in the middle of the gallery, alone.

I then made my way over to a table with a couple of dozen glasses of wine laid out in neat rows. I then picked up a glass and started drinking. Within the next half-hour I consumed somewhere in the neighborhood of five or six glasses (I lost count). In between sips, I observed the crowd mingling in little bunches of three and four, ignoring the art. After realizing that if I drank much more I wouldn't be able to make it home, I walked out.

About a month later I summoned the courage to call Leo and ask about future exhibits. I thought I might also ask about a one person show featuring my paintings. Again, it took several calls to get him on the phone, but finally he answered my call.

"Hi Emma, what can I do for you?"

"I just wanted to check in and see what your future plans were. I mean, of course, what should I plan for in terms of future exhibits?"

"Yes, good idea," he began. "I hope your work is going well. I assume that New York is inspiring a lot of great work."

"Yes indeed," I lied. "I'm working hard." Actually, so far, seeing all the shows in literally dozens of galleries in New York, had inspired the exact opposite reaction. There were so many artists, doing so much work of such variety, that I started to feel that there was simply no way to be noticed in such a crowded environment. It actually discouraged my efforts. To make matters worse, everyone seemed to be working in styles that were totally foreign to what I wanted to do.

"That's great to hear," he chirped. "As far as future plans are concerned, I have good news. We have another group show coming up in March. I'm really excited about it. We have some great artists lined up for that show, and you are definitely on that list. Just send over a couple of your latest paintings in February and we'll take a look. I'm sure they will work well for that show.

Another group show four months from now. I felt totally deflated, but I decided that, at least at this point, I better not ask about a one person show. That possibility sounded out of the question. I reminded myself that a lot of artists don't even have a gallery. I had to remain patient.

"Great, that sounds good," I replied, in as upbeat a tone as I could muster. "I'll send over a couple of paintings in February."

"Great Emma. Good talking to you. Sorry, I have to go." And just like before, the phone went dead before I could even say goodbye.

I stuck to my routine over that cold winter, working at the diner, painting, visiting shows. In February, as promised, I chose two paintings, and took them over to the gallery. Leo wasn't in the gallery at the time, so one of his assistants took the paintings. She took one glance at them, and then looked at me like I was a total lost cause, and that was about the way I felt.

When the show opened, I was again included, but as before, Leo found an obscure back wall for my work. Again, I tried to look on the bright side. At least I was included. At least I had made it into two shows in New York in my first year in the city. That was way ahead of a lot of artists.

Chapter 22

How I Became a Minimalist

In April, I called Leo and told him that I wanted to make an appointment to see him. I began to have this feeling that my days of being included in Leo's shows were numbered. I reasoned that I had better take action quickly, or I would soon be without a gallery. He tried to take care of what I needed over the phone, telling me several times that his schedule was packed this time of year, but I insisted. I wanted to sit down with him and have a meeting. "I need to discuss a couple of things with you, and I think it would be best if we met."

He finally agreed. "Let me see, maybe we can meet next Tuesday. No, that won't work. How about week after next on Wednesday?"

I agreed, and was standing outside his office at the appointed time. When I got there, he was on the phone. I waited. I wasn't going anywhere. After a half-hour he leaned out the door of his office and said, "Sorry, I have to take care of this. A collector. Do you want to reschedule? This might take awhile."

"No, I'll wait."

He looked disappointed, but agreed to talk to me as soon as he was able to wrap up this pressing issue. After an hour, he finally ushered me into his office and asked me to take a seat.

"What can I do for you," he began, in a tone that clearly indicated an impatience with having his valuable time taken up by a frumpy female artist who's paintings don't sell.

I began as diplomatically as I could. "I appreciate the fact that you have included my paintings in two group shows this year. I appreciate the exposure, but I expected a little more. When you invited me to come to New York, and show my work in your gallery, I thought that meant that you would feature my work a little more prominently. Maybe I was being a little naive, but at this point, I have to ask you what your future plans are? Do you plan to exhibit more of my paintings more prominently?"

He adjusted uncomfortably in his seat, with a frown on his face. "Listen Emma, I know it doesn't seem like much, but I'm trying to run a business here. I have to feature a variety of work. Collectors have different tastes. Every artist who walks in here wants their work to be front and center all the time. I just can't do that and stay in business. Your work hasn't sold."

He paused to let that uncomfortable fact settle in before he continued. "Believe me, I love your work. I wouldn't have invited you to New York if I didn't like what I saw. But one of the reasons that I wanted you to come to the city was so that you could see what was going on, what the latest trends were. Have you looked around the galleries to see what other artists are doing right now?"

I said that I had. "Then you must be aware of the problem. You're working in an Abstract Expressionist style. Don't get me wrong, I love Abstract Expressionism. When I first started my gallery, more than ten years ago, Abstract Expressionism was all the rage. When I first saw your work in Santa Fe, there was still an interest in the Abstract Expressionists. Yes, the Pop artists were starting to make a splash, but there was still a lot of interest in Abstract Expressionism.

"Now, I'm sorry to say, that is over. The 1970s are all about Minimalism. In fact, from what I'm hearing from the critics, we may be looking at a period that painting dies altogether. I hope that doesn't happen. I still hold out hope, but there are many out there saying that painting is dead. I'm sorry, but that's simply the reality. Collectors aren't interested in Abstract Expressionism from an unknown artist. If you were one of the original innovators in that movement then, maybe, I could still sell your work. What collectors are looking for now is all this new Minimalist stuff."

I knew what he was trying to say to me. Every gallery I visited was showing Minimalist art. A lot of this stuff was showing up in museums as well, and I had to admit that a lot of what I was seeing was very good, or at least very interesting. This was the time that artists like Sol LeWitt, John Baldessari, Antonio Caro, Frank Stella, Donald Judd, Agnes Martin, Dan Flavin, and Robert Morris, were all active and monopolizing the attention of the art world. I just couldn't identify with a lot of this work. It just didn't feel like it was right for me. That fact bothered me a lot, but I kept thinking that if I did what seemed right for me, people out there would see that, and appreciate the fact that I was staying true to myself.

Of course, that was naive, and I realized that fact as Leo lectured me on what was selling now. I promised to reassess my work and, hopefully, move toward something that was more appealing for his collectors. That seemed to brighten his spirits immensely, and he quickly wrapped up the meeting and ushered me out of his office.

Over the next several months I tried all kinds of new approaches to painting, all of which I found unsatisfactory in one way or another. I finally settled on paintings that consisted of large squares of color with pieces of scrap wood attached to the canvas. Since painting seemed to be in decline, I reasoned that maybe I could go halfway, and combine painting with sculptural elements. Soon I was creating works of art that looked like a cross between a Louise Nevelson sculpture and a Mark Rothko painting.

Before the fall group show, I brought several of these new creations into the gallery and set them against a wall. Leo came out of his office when he heard that I had come in with some new paintings. As soon as he was in front of them I saw him wince, but he maintained his usual diplomatic aplomb that every good gallery owner employs on a daily basis.

"Interesting Emma, very interesting," he began. "Yes, I can see that you are experimenting with something quite new." He continued to study the paintings with a concentrated expression. "Yes, it's good to try new ideas, and you're moving toward the potential for something quite original. Yes, I think you're moving in the right direction."

Of course, I knew what that meant. He thought they were awful, but he didn't want to discourage me. I had to agree with his assessment, but this was as Minimalist as I could get. To keep me going, he did display them in his next group show in October. I think he felt guilty about luring me to New York. Or, maybe he just felt sorry for me and decided that it wouldn't hurt to stick them in a back corner of the gallery, which is exactly where they went. As usual, I attended the opening, searched for the hidden spot that he had placed my paintings, and once I found them, headed for the wine bar, and drank as much as possible before I left.

After that "experiment" failed miserably, I became obsessed with my backgrounds. In a way, I reasoned, Minimalist paintings are usually just one or two solid colors. Many of these minimalist paintings looked as if the artist covered the canvas with a background color, and then forgot to paint anything else on top of the background.

That led me to begin to concentrate all my energy into creating a background that seemed to be one solid color, but if you looked closer the colors gradually changed as the eye moved across the canvas. I wanted the color changes to be so subtle, and so gradual, that the viewer was barely aware of the change. I also wanted to make the viewer work hard in order to see the change. If someone came into the gallery and took just a quick glance, I wanted them to miss the changes. I also wanted this background to seem translucent. If a viewer stood in front of the canvas long enough, I wanted them to begin to think that they could almost look through the surface of the canvas into some dark inner world.

For the final touch on these new paintings, I added very thin, hard-edged lines streaming down the canvas, no more than an eight of an inch wide. Sometimes, these lines extended almost the entire length of the painting. At other times, they were only three of four inches long.

Sometimes I might put a dozen or more of these lines on a painting. On other canvases, there might be only four of five.

I worked hard to make the placement of the lines at various spots on the canvas seem totally random. I didn't want the viewer to think that there was a pattern to where each of these lines were placed. I always chose to paint these lines with very bold colors - red, gold, even orange. My goal was to make sure the lines were in complete contrast to the dark background.

I called these paintings, 'Random Lines,' and then added a number to each one - Random Lines One, Random Lines Two, etc. These titles helped. The Minimalists liked titles that referred to the process, or to the abstract quality of the work. In fact, when I took them to the gallery, and one of the assistants heard the titles, she immediately commented that I must be working with some of the same ideas as Sol LeWitt. Of course, she was referring to the fact that he would develop a formula, and the execution of the formula would create the painting.

Actually, I wasn't thinking of LeWitt at all. His ideas were all about creating a conceptual idea, and letting assistants actually execute, or create, the painting. I felt that my work was very much a product of my skill as an artist, especially my backgrounds. But after she made that statement, I agreed that there was a connection, and that she was very perceptive to take note of that. I knew that by relating my work to one of the biggest names in Minimalist art the staff of the gallery would see my work as more relevant.

If I had been able to choose what I wanted to paint, I doubt I would have ever done these paintings, but since I had to come up with something resembling Minimalism, these paintings seemed as close as I was going to get. After I mastered my technique, producing just the right effect for the background, I really liked several of these compositions.

When Leo saw them he seemed to respond in a much more affirmative way. He actually asked one of his young assistants to come over and take a look when I brought them in for the March group show. When the show opened, I was totally surprised. The paintings were in the main part of the gallery, and were actually visible from the entrance, and he put up three paintings rather than the usual two.

Then, about a month after the show opened, I was really shocked when I got a call from the gallery. They informed me that one of my paintings had actually sold for $4,000, and I was to receive $2,000 from the purchase. That was a lot of money back in the 1970s. When Leo called me about the purchase he said that the collector who bought it thought that the background looked like fog or mist, and the lines seemed to him to be raindrops falling from the sky. Leo laughed. "I couldn't bear to tell him that the painting is really about random distribution of structural lines."

I laughed along with Leo. I wanted to let him postulate whatever he wanted to think, as long as that encouraged him to try to sell my paintings. But I actually liked the interpretation of the collector. Maybe he was a little naive, and not up on the latest Minimalist theories, but I thought his way of seeing the painting was interesting, and I felt that because of that interpretation he"ll probably enjoy the painting a lot more than if he had been fully versed on the latest aesthetic theories.

After the minor success of these latest paintings, I thought that Leo might give me a one-person show. I should have known better. Although he now took my phone calls a little more promptly, and was much more positive in our conversations, over the next year the only reward I received for painting Minimalist canvases was a more prominent spot in his group shows. But, I couldn't complain. He actually succeeded in selling two more of my paintings that were in those group exhibits.

Then, after three years in New York, I got a call from a friend who asked me if I heard that the gallery was closing. I was totally taken aback. I immediately took a cab down to the gallery to see for myself. Sure enough, the gallery was locked up, and no one was around. I tried to call Leo for the next three days, but no one answered. I eventually learned that the gallery had never done well financially, and that he had turned to other investments to try to make up the difference. He wound up loosing a lot of money on a risky financial speculation, and that had sent him into bankruptcy. I wasn't even able to recover the five paintings I had in the gallery at the time it closed.

After Leo's gallery closed I tried to find another that would take my work. I must have walked into thirty galleries over the next six months. No one was interested. A few gallery owners took a look at my work, and a couple even said they would keep me in mind for the future, but nothing came of it.

At the same time it was becoming harder and harder to continue to paint what I had been working on. My Random Line paintings had been at least somewhat successful, and I wound up creating probably two dozen works in this series, but after awhile I began to feel that I couldn't keep replicating the same formula over and over again. There were just so many variations and combinations of random lines over a dark background that I could invent. I felt like I really needed to develop something new, or at least something that was somewhat different than these paintings. Increasingly, with each painting session, I found myself doing a lot more staring at a blank canvas than actual painting.

Chapter 23

I Face the Inevitable

There is an old Bernstein song about artists and musicians coming to New York to try to make it big and ultimately failing. And there's one line from that song that resonated with me so much at about this time. At one point in the song the line is, "Go back to Ohio." Well, I didn't go back to Ohio, I did something worse, I went back to Texas. While I had been trying to establish myself in New York Gary's life had taken a number of interesting turns.

After one year at McMurry College, he dropped out and found a job in construction in Wichita Falls, Texas. No more than three months after he left school, he got his girlfriend pregnant. Of course, they were forced to get married as quickly as possible. As you might expect, I didn't get an invitation to the wedding. Gary reasoned that traveling from New York was just too much to ask. I pointed out to him that, in this day and age, we had jet airplanes that could deliver me there in just a few hours. He didn't see the humor or the sarcasm in my comment.

Shortly after the first baby came, Carol got pregnant again. Within three years, when he was barely twenty-two years old, he had two young children. If that wasn't enough, Carol, who suffered from asthma, had developed a severe case of pneumonia.

When I had a conversation with him on the phone, he talked a lot about how wonderful the kids were, but he complained about how difficult it had been trying to manage his job responsibilities, take care of the kids, and help Carol recover. "Carol is really feeling overwhelmed," he said, and went on at length about how tired she was.

During a period when both the kids had been sick, and Carol was exhausted from trying to manage her own illness, I took a chance and suggested to him that I could come down and stay for awhile and help take care of the children. I explained that I really had nothing to gain by remaining in New York right now. I finished by saying that I could work on my paintings just as easily in Texas as in New York, although that wasn't really true.

His response was cordial but not very positive. He even commented at one point that he thought my coming down wouldn't be a good idea. Yet, by the end of the conversation, he agreed to talk to Carol about the situation and let me know what she thought. It seemed clear that Gary wasn't that excited about the idea of me being in the same house with his family. Carol, on the other hand, had no negative history with me, and the thing that was most on her mind at that point was finding some way of getting a break from the overwhelming job of taking care of two small kids. It didn't take long to get a response from her. In fact, instead of hearing back from Gary, just a day later Carol herself called, and said she would love to have me come down to help out while she was recovering.

"It would be great to have you nearby. I could really use a little help with the kids. They can be a lot to handle, and I just need a break from time to time."

I told her I completely understood. "I know what you're going through. I had the same experience with my own kids. Young children are wonderful, but they can also be totally exhausting. I wasn't even sick. You"re dealing with an illness on top of everything else."

"Then you understand my situation," she said.

"Yes," I immediately replied, "and I would love to come down and help out. It's the least I can do. It will also give me a chance to get to know the kids. I don't like being so far away from my grandchildren."

It was very clear that Carol couldn't wait for me to arrive. As far as she was concerned, the sooner I got there the better. Gary, on the other hand, was much less excited, but I think that he concluded that he had better not challenge Carol on this one. She needed help with the kids, and it was clear that I could be of assistance.

Initially, I thought I might just stay with them in their house, but I soon thought better of that idea. From comments Gary made, as I formulated my plans for the move, I could tell he wasn't at all exited about me being close to his family. After one particularly sharp comment from Gary, I knew that I had better find somewhere to go to give them some space from time to time.

Shortly after I arrived in Texas, I found a small studio a little over a mile from their house. Although small according to Texas standards, it seemed spacious in comparison with the place I had in New York. As soon as I was up and running in my new apartment, I was helping Carol take care of the kids on a regular basis. On many a day I was also nursing her, which seemed to bring us together. She and I soon were on very friendly terms, and I made a point of being the well behaved mother-in-law. I always made an effort to support Carol in any way I could. I never criticized her, and I tried to stay away when I sensed that she and Gary wanted time alone.

As time went by, we did a lot together. We even sometimes prepared meals and took the kids to the playground together. In fact, with time, Carol began to open up to me, sometimes asking me for advise, and on occasion telling me personal things about herself. But she never talked about Gary. I think she realized that our relationship was troubled, and I'm sure that Gary had told her that I had abandoned the family. I think she was afraid that if she said anything about him, or their marriage, Gary would see it as a betrayal.

Gary still maintained his distance from me. He was always cordial, and went through the motions of welcoming me whenever I came over to the house to take care of the kids, but we never talked intimately. I could never pierce a thick layer he had built up, although I continuously searched for an opening. He seemed to have buried his emotions and his anger about his childhood experiences deep inside himself. As an adult he had become a reserved man who rarely spoke more than a few words. He detested people who talked a lot and could become agitated just by being around them.

At times, I felt so hungry for a closer connection that I considered simply confronting him and telling him I wanted to talk about our relationship, about the past, about why we were so distant from each other now. But every time I came close to saying something I lost my courage and kept quiet. The one time that I brought up our relationship was when his boy started acting up, and Gary got angry with him.

"You may not remember, but you could have your moods when you were a boy," I said. He stopped suddenly and stared at me without saying a word. I suddenly felt very uncomfortable, but at the same time I thought I might have the opportunity at this point to get him to talk to me about our relationship.

I began carefully. "You know, that's one of the things you discover once you have grandchildren. You get to compare both your children and your grandchildren to each other. They often seem to repeat many of the same characteristics. I see your son as a lot like you. I know you might not want to hear that right now, when you're having discipline issues with him, but it's true. He's just like you in many ways," I said with a slight laugh.

He obviously didn't see my comment as in the slightest way funny. "Are you telling me that he's as difficult to deal with as I was," he said, with a tone that seemed on the border of open anger. "Is this your way of showing me why you didn't want to take care of me. I guess you think that, since I'm having difficulty with my son, I'll understand what you suffered." His voice grew angrier by the second. "The only difference is that I'm not going to walk out on my son like you walked out on both of yours."

I was stunned. I didn't think that what I had said had been in the least bit controversial. His reaction seemed completely out of proportion to the situation. Something, maybe the fact that he was trying to figure out how to deal with his son's rebelliousness, caused old anger, stored up against me, to bubble to the surface.

"I didn't mean that at all," I cried. "You must understand that your behavior as a child had nothing to do with me leaving. I loved you just the way you were. The reason I left was because of my relationship with your father. We couldn't make our marriage work."

"And you wanted to go off and live the life of a carefree artist," he hissed. "That was so much more interesting than being with your boring and difficult to handle kids," he replied with words that felt as sharp as needles pricking the skin.

"It's not that simple," I replied. "I never wanted to leave. Yes, I wanted to be an artist, but I didn't want to leave either you or your brother. But your father wouldn't allow me to do what I needed to do to become an artist. I tried to work out a suitable arrangement with him, but he wouldn't hear of it. He didn't understand what it meant to me, and at times he was totally hostile toward my work."

"That's enough!" he commanded. "I don't want to have this conversation."

"I just wanted to try to explain what happened," I whispered. I just wanted to ..." I stuttered, trying to find the words. "I was just trying to show, to somehow convince you that it wasn't you or your brother that made me leave. I loved both of you."

"I said I don't want to have this conversation, and I meant it," he yelled. He then pivoted around, knocking a table over as he exited the room.

That was the last time we ever came close to discussing the past and his childhood experiences. From then on I steered clear of any mention of his childhood, and I was careful to never compare my experience raising him with his experience raising his children. Also, by the time this conversation took place, Carol was beginning to feel a lot better. They didn't need grandma around to take care of the children quite as much. I suspect that Gary was perfectly happy that I wasn't coming over as much.

About six months after my arrival in Wichita Falls I got a call from Don in Santa Fe. He had heard that I was back in the Southwest, and he thought he would check up and see how I was doing. At this point, since Carol seemed to be doing much better, I had thought about returning to New York, but I couldn't get excited about it. I started doing some temp work, mainly typing jobs for various businesses around town. Since I had once worked for two law firms, I had found some temporary positions in a local law firm.

"I forgot that you used to work in a law firm," Don said. "You know, there's a lawyer here in Santa Fe who bought several of my paintings for his offices. I could give him a call and see if he needs a top-notch secretary who is also a big-shot New York artist."

"I don't know Don," I replied. "I don't know if I could work in an office that had your paintings on all the walls," I joked.

"Very funny," he snickered.

"Seriously, I'll give him a call and see what he says."

"I don't know Don," I repeated. "I'm not sure I want to stay down here. I was planning on going back to New York."

"But it sounds like you need to stay down here in case your son's family needs help. Listen, I'll give this lawyer a call and see what he says. Who knows if he'll even have a job opening. If he does, it won't hurt to talk to him. You don't necessarily have to stay there forever. If you're in Santa Fe, it means you can be closer to your family. Later, if they don't need you around, you can always go back to the big city. I'm sure New York isn't going to go away."

I deeply suspected, in fact I knew, that he wanted to renew our relationship. If I came back to Santa Fe I was certain that he felt he could lure me back into his clutches. I was reluctant to put myself in a position where I would be forced to fight off his advances, but I finally agreed to let him call this friend of his. At this point I just couldn't face going back to New York and trying to get myself into another gallery.

Don called me back two days later and told me that his lawyer friend wanted to talk to me, so I drove to Santa Fe for the interview. It had been almost five years since I had been in New Mexico, but everything seemed to be exactly the same.

When I arrived in town I checked into a downtown hotel, and before I could unpack my suitcase, the phone rang. I could tell that Don was very excited for me to be back, and he offered to take me to dinner. I was really tired, but I felt like I really couldn't say no.

During dinner he caught me up on all the local gossip, and told me that he was sure that his gallery would welcome me back. "I'm not so sure," I told him. "My style has changed drastically since I left Santa Fe. Everyone's doing Minimalism in the city right now, and I guess I felt like I had to follow the wave and go in that direction as well."

"I wouldn't worry about it," Don replied. "I'm sure Frank will be more than happy to show anything you've done. Just yesterday he told me that he would love to have you back. He said that, 'When I tell everyone that she's a hot-shot New York artist, people around here will really be excited.' So you see, your time in New York will give you celebrity status with all the collectors."

"I'm not so sure anyone here will like what I'm doing now," I commented hesitantly. "My paintings are somewhat conceptual now, which I feel fairly certain is not going to appeal to Santa Fe collectors."

"Wow," he exclaimed. "I can't wait to see this stuff. It sounds really radical."

After dinner Don was sending all kinds of signals, flirting as much as possible, but that was the last thing I was looking for at this point. I finally told him that I was totally exhausted after the trip and needed to get some sleep. He finally got the hint and departed.

The next day I went to my interview and, sure enough, Don's paintings were on every wall. Samuel Goggins, the head of the firm, and the admirer of Don's paintings, conducted the interview. He led me around, showing me each of Don's canvases, explaining different aspects of each painting, like I wasn't already thoroughly familiar with Don's work. You could tell he was very proud of his collection.

After a brief discussion I was hired on the spot. Clearly, after Don had talked to him, I probably could have come in and stood on my head and still been offered a job. I even began to wonder if Don had offered him a painting, or some other enticement, in order to get me hired. But the firm seemed like a good place to work, and I felt like I would be very comfortable working for Mr. Goggins, so I accepted the position and made plans to move back to Santa Fe.

I rented an apartment the next day and settled back into life in New Mexico. Within a week Frank called me and asked if I would be interested in showing my new paintings in his gallery. I was sure that Don had talked to him. I told him that at this time I was taking a break and wasn't working on anything new.

"What about the paintings you were doing in New York? Are any of those available?"

"Well, I'm having them shipped from New York. If you want to see them when they arrive, I guess you can take a look at them, but I doubt you'll be interested in what I was doing there."

When they arrived I brought a few over to his gallery. He looked at each one, studying them carefully. "I don't understand what's going on here. These paintings are so different than what you were doing before. Wow, you really changed your style while you were in New York."

"Yes, I guess I did," I replied. He kept looking at the paintings, scratching his chin, and shifting from one foot to the other.

"Minimalism is what all the artists are doing in New York right now. So I went that direction in my work."

I could tell that he didn't know what to do with these paintings, but he honored his invitation and showed them in his gallery for about six months. Of course, none of them sold, and I eventually suggested that he return them to me since there wasn't any interest in this kind of work. I think he was relieved. That was my last involvement with an art gallery for a number of years.

In the first few weeks after I arrived, the phone kept ringing with Don invariably on the other end of the line. "Would you like to go to dinner? Would you like to go see an exhibit?" He was so enthusiastic, and so persistent. He made it very clear that he wanted to renew our old relationship, but I just couldn't do it. At this point in my life, the last thing I wanted was a man, especially a man who was an artist. After everything that had happened over the last couple of years, I wanted to get away from art and men. I wanted to climb into a protective cave and somehow try to clear my mind.

Chapter 24

My Return to Art

When I left New York I was a little burned out and discouraged. Obviously, my attempt to make it big in the art world had not gone according to plan. On the other hand, those four years had been an incredibly rich period of learning and exploration. I had absorbed so much about art, how the art world worked, and how important art intersected with a deep intellectual and philosophical realm.

Yet, at the same time, I was mentally drained, and felt that I still hadn't found my way as an artist. I somehow wasn't able to find and mix and blend the right ingredients to create that special dish that nourishes the mind and the soul and the body. My New York experience had made me realize that I might not ever find the right combination of ingredients necessary to make the kind of art I so hoped to create. I had seen so many people valiantly struggling, desperately searching for that elusive mixture called great art, and I knew that most wouldn't find it. Now, I had to face the very real possibility that I was one of those people.

So I stopped creating art. I tried to stop thinking about art, although I never quite pulled that off. In short, I tried to refocus my life. I delved into my new job with determination. I used work as a way of finding a new self, but also an escape. I can't say that it was totally successful. There were times in the middle of the night that I would lay in bed, unable to sleep, and yearn to pick up a brush, to mix paints, and attack a canvas. But I resisted these forces deep inside me.

I felt that I had to stay away from art, explore another way of being, look away from art, and then maybe, at some point in the future, I could return and locate a truly unique vision. I knew that special vision might never come, but if I went back to painting too quickly, I was sure old patterns would emerge, the demands of the market would force themselves into my mind, and truly original art would again submerge itself, and never float back to the surface.

I told Don that, as nice as he was, and as much as I cared for him, I just couldn't renew our old relationship. I just couldn't do it. He was hurt and deeply wounded by my rejection. For several months he wouldn't accept what I made painfully clear, but eventually he gave up trying to coax me back. Occasionally, we ran into each other, it was almost unavoidable, but each time it happened his face took on the visage of deep distress and pain. We did our best to remain cordial but escape each other as quickly as possible.

Then, about two years after I had returned to Santa Fe, Don suffered a stroke and died immediately. It happened while he was giving a lecture to one of his classes at the University. I was stunned, and I must admit I felt a little guilty when I heard of his death. I thought that, maybe I should have given in and renewed our relationship. But with time I realized that, if I had done that, I probably would have made his last two years miserable. No, the way things had turned out had been for the best.

About a year after Don passed, Gary called me and told me that Mel had died. Gary was very upset, more upset than I had ever seen him. He had worshipped his father to the end. It was like he didn't want to see what his father was really like. The circumstances of his father's death made the whole experience even worse for his son. Mel had died of a drug overdose. I have to say that I wasn't surprised. Mel was always looking for cheap thrills wherever he could find them. But Gary was shocked. He couldn't believe his father had been using drugs.

Throughout these years I continued to work for the Santa Fe law firm that had hired me at Don's insistence. Samuel was a good boss. He was always congenial, and was appreciative of the work I did. Since I didn't have much of a social life, I was always willing to work a little overtime when things got really busy. He was always so appreciative of my willingness to do whatever was needed in the office. About two years after I began working there he promoted me to office manager, and I continued in that role until I retired. In all, I wound up working for his firm for twenty-two years, twenty as office manager.

A year after I had become office manager of the firm I decided that it was finally time for me to visit Europe. Here I was, forty-seven years old, and I had never been to the continent. Now, for the first time, my income was good enough to make the trip if I was careful with my money. I asked Samuel for an extra week of vacation, and off I went.

On this first trip I visited France, Germany, Switzerland, and wound up my excursion in Italy. It was a whirlwind tour, and by the end of my three weeks I realized that this wasn't the best way to see Europe. Although this first trip served to introduce me to the wonders Europe had to offer, I realized that if I was going to really gain anything from my short time there I had to take a different approach.

The next year, when I took my three week vacation, I chose one city, Paris, to visit, and, except for a couple of short excursions to places close to the city, I stayed in Paris for the whole length of my trip. I tried to immerse myself in the city, absorbing the culture as deeply as I could, and I haunted the wonderful museums for which Paris is known.

The following year, I visited Vienna for the entire three weeks, and in addition to frequent visits to the museums, I attended an opera or a concert almost every night. Vienna is the finest city in the world for operas and classical music, and I took full advantage of what the city offered during my stay.

I always chose to go to Europe the week of Thanksgiving, returning in mid-December. That was when the firm's business dropped off somewhat, and it was a time that American tourists didn't overwhelm the continent. In subsequent years I visited other cities and countries.

I couldn't make it every year, but I went whenever I could, visiting a different place each trip.

When I retired in 1996, one of the first things I did was head for Europe. But this time I didn't limit myself to three weeks. I had saved enough money to make a much lengthier stay overseas, and wound up living in Paris for almost five months. The following year I spent four months in Munich, with side trips to Salzburg, Zurich, and several other cities. I couldn't afford to make these extended stays every year on my retirement income, but in the sixteen years since I retired I have been able to make six trips lasting from two to five months.

These trips to Europe proved invaluable for finding my way back to art. New York had been a revelation. I learned so much while I was there. But New York is really a young city. It's energy and enthusiasm comes from jumping on whatever the next wave happens to be. New York never looks back, and that's both its strength and its weakness.

Europe is layered. Historic periods exist in close proximity, bumping up against one another. You can see it in its architecture. In so many European cities, a modern building is next to a nineteenth century building, which is next to a sixteenth century building, which is next to something from the Middle Ages. And they don't seem to clash. They actually reinforce one another. Europe is a rich stew of centuries of cultural accumulation. As Henry James so eloquently put it, "Europe is ever so many things at once, not only beauty and art and supreme design, but history and fame and power, the world in fine raised to the richest and noblest expression."

That realization, which took me some time to really understand, wound up proving absolutely essential when I took up painting again. I came to see that I didn't have to ride the latest cultural wave. Yes, it was important to know what was going on in the most up-to-date galleries, to understand what the latest aesthetic theories brought to the table, and what the insights artists practicing the newest fads were offering us. But a deep understanding of historical styles, an ability to see the interrelated threads of different periods in art, was just as important. Maybe, when one came to truly understand these historical periods, that depth of knowledge gave you the tools to do something truly new, truly original.

I eventually started thinking about picking up my brushes again. They say that timing is everything, and I guess my timing was particularly bad. Literally one year after I left New York, the artist Susan Rothenberg was given her first solo exhibition at the 112 Green Street Gallery. This gallery exhibited just three large paintings by Rothenberg, but they changed the course of the New York art scene in a single blow.

With these three paintings, she broke out of the Minimalist mode and reintroduced figuration to painting. She also employed painterly gestures that harkened back to the Abstract Expressionists. All of a sudden painters could do what painters loved to do, and that was to paint. By 1980, an entire movement, known as Neo-expressionism, was dominating the New York gallery scene, and Minimalism, that had so monopolized the art world when I was in the city, was over.

I thought to myself at the time that if I had landed in New York in 1980, rather than 1970, my tale as a new artist in the city might have been very different. Although I was bitter, even disgusted with the art world's inability to see and appreciate art that might not fit into the latest fad, seeing these changes gave me the inspiration to return to painting. In 1982, on my way to Europe on one of my three week vacations, I stopped by New York, and made my way around to the galleries that were showing the Neo-expressionists. What I saw made me itch to get back to my easel.

Although, with a full-time job, it was hard to find time to paint, within a year I had produced about a dozen paintings. In 1984, Frank began to show my paintings again in his gallery, and over the course of the 1980s I did very well. This was the time when, due to generous tax incentives, corporations were buying large numbers of paintings. I must have sold at least two dozen paintings during this period. In fact, my sales during the 1980s funded a couple of my trips to Europe. But as soon as the tax laws changed, corporations stopped buying, and the phone stopped ringing. I went back to the usual lot for artists like me, one or two sales a year, if I was lucky.

Connections with my family settled into a sporadic condition marked by an occasional visit with Gary's family at Christmas time. In mid-December, usually right after I returned from Europe, I would give Gary a call and ask them what they were doing for Christmas. Quite often, they were going to Carol's parent's house for the holiday. But occasionally, for one reason or another, that plan wasn't working out, so I would ask if I could join them. He never invited me, but I would brazenly coax him into letting me come. I would go on about not having seen the grandkids in ages, and he would eventually give in to my pleas. But I knew not to stay more than a very short time, and I think my longest visit was not more than three days.

Of course, by the mid 1990s, the kids were grown and were out living active lives, so I rarely received an invitation to visit. I call Gary once every few months, just to find out what everyone is doing. Usually, the calls are very short. I can tell that Gary really doesn't enjoy talking with me that much. He isn't much of a talker anyway.

By the mid 1980s, Gary had settled his family in Lubbock. From the time I had helped take care of the kids, back in 1974, until he finally found a job that he stayed with for more than a year or two, in 1983, Gary had moved from job to job. He finally found a position in a grocery store, and that's where he continued to work. Now he's just a few years away from retirement. His kids are now in their forties and have kids of their own. One still lives in Lubbock and works as a car salesman. The other lives in Dallas and works as a store clerk.

With that, I think I've come to the end of my story. There isn't much more that I can tell you that would fill out the story much more, and it's getting very late.

Chapter 25

There's Nothing Like the Child of an Artist

After Emma finished telling me her fascinating tale I thanked her for her willingness to be so honest. The next day she left New York and went back home. I promised to update her on the progress we made preparing the exhibit, and told her that I hoped to schedule the show in the next four to six months. She thanked me for spending so much time talking with her. I assured her that the pleasure was all mine.

After she left, I got right to work on putting her show together. I spent a lot of time studying the twenty or so paintings she had sent to the gallery, always thinking about how I could curate her work in the best possible way. I spent a lot of time thinking about how to market her art, but more importantly, how to market her, how to sell her unique story.

Collectors, when they are investing thousands, or in some cases, hundreds of thousands, in a painting or sculpture, are very concerned about the reputation of the artist. Most aren't simply purchasing something decorative to hang in their house. No, their first priority is buying art as an investment. I wish so much that this wasn't our current situation. It so distorts the appreciation of art in my humble estimation. The dizzying amounts of money being thrown around can sometimes get into the head of artists and lead them astray. That's the sad reality we live with today.

I eventually concluded that the best way to present Emma was as an artist doing dynamic and incredible work in the final phase of her career, someone who's been creating original work for many years, but now was putting all that experience together in one last golden era. I felt that all I needed was a period of two to three years to build her reputation to a level that museum curators would start taking her seriously and ultimately purchasing her work for their museums.

Then, approximately two months after her visit, everything fell apart. I got a call late one afternoon, just before I was leaving for the day. Quite without warning, Emma had suffered a stroke and died immediately. I was totally stunned. She seemed to be in such good health when she visited.

Her son Gary made the call. His tone, based on what she had told me about him, was just what I expected. His explanation of what had happened was very smooth and calm. There was absolutely no emotion in his voice whatsoever. His speech sounded soft, an even baritone, a strong Southern accent delivered very dry and distant. I could tell that he viewed this whole conversation as simply the business that had to be addressed in situations like this.

He suggested that, since I had a number of Emma's paintings at the gallery, and had been planning an exhibit of her work, it might be best if he traveled to New York in order to meet with me. I agreed wholeheartedly, and suggested that he come to the city as soon as he could. We made an appointment for the following week.

After the phone call, I immediately walked to the back room where we had stored Emma's paintings and pulled everyone of them out. I looked over each one separately with deep emotion. These paintings were so strong, so unique, so beautiful. After hearing her story, and knowing that she was now gone, the paintings resonated even more convincingly as a testament to her struggle against all that life had thrown at her. Each painting was concrete proof that she had fought valiantly against the forces that had arrayed against her. I felt that, in the end, she had triumphed, that ultimately she had won the battle against a soul killing universe.

When her son arrived the next week I welcomed him into my office and offered him a seat on a couch that sat at the opposite end of the room from my desk. I wanted him to feel comfortable and at ease. I took a seat in the chair at a right angle to the couch. As we were taking our seats my assistant rushed into the room and asked if he would like tea, coffee, or water. He refused everything.

I could tell that he clearly saw this visit as a very formal business meeting and was not interested in chitchat or informalities of any kind. He was dressed in a cheap, ill-fitting suit, that tended to bunch up around the shoulders and neck. I could see that he wasn't used to wearing suits, and I guessed that this was probably his only one. He was somewhat overweight and was rapidly going bald. He moved slowly and deliberately.

The first thought that came into my mind as we sat down was how different he was from Emma. If I met him on the street I would have never suspected that he could possibly be related to Emma. They seemed so different in almost every way. She had been a bundle of energy, thin and very attractive, sharp and easygoing. She was the height of sophistication, he seemed the very embodiment of what one would classify as a boorish rustic. He seemed slow and cumbersome, almost robotic when he spoke.

I began the conversation. "I first want to say how sorry I am to hear of Emma's passing. In the short time I knew her, I enjoyed her company immensely, and grew to really appreciate her unique charm. I really enjoyed talking to her. She was so knowledgeable about art, and I really liked her work. She was so smart, but also very humble. Those characteristics, I must say, are not that common in artists. Artists can have an oversized ego," I said jokingly.

He didn't seem to understand my comment as just the light, offhand remark of a gallery owner. "Yes, I can see that you in your position must have to deal with selfish artists constantly. I can assure you, knowing my mother, that's one thing that I'm already well aware of."

I adjusted uncomfortably in my seat and decided that I had better change the tone and direction of my remarks. Unlike his mother, Emma's son was not one to engage in friendly banter.

"I just want to begin and say that your mother's art is really excellent. I truly believe that a number of her paintings are absolutely superb and compare favorably with anything we have in the gallery. In fact, I would be willing to place her work alongside any artist in New York. Although her death makes it hard for me to implement my original plan, namely, to introduce her to the New York art scene as an artist working in a final late-in-life burst of creative genius, I still hope that I can bring favorable attention to her work."

I paused a minute to try to gauge his reaction, but his face betrayed no feeling one way or another. "Of course, galleries like mine rarely feature the work of artists no longer living, and usually, when they do, it is the work of major figures who have a known reputation. Galleries, unlike art museums, are usually dedicated to the idea of presenting the next new talent, and that means that usually, when we introduce a new artist, they are fairly young, or at least not past mid-career. It will be an uphill battle for me to successfully bring your mother's art the kind of attention I had hoped to foster, but I want to assure you that I believe in your mother's work so passionately that I am willing to give it my best effort."

I leaned forward in order to emphasize what I had to say next. "So this is what I propose. I would like to mount an exhibit of your mother's work within the next six months. If that exhibit is successful, and I'm able to succeed in stirring up at least a little interest, I will follow up with another exhibit next year. Hopefully, that will get the ball rolling, and we can then assess where we stand and plan our next move after that."

I hesitated a moment to let these ideas soak in before I continued. "But in order to make this project successful I need more of her work. She sent me about twenty of her paintings. That was enough for one show. I didn't ask for more since, of course, I expected her to create more work over the next year. As you might imagine, I felt that her second show with us would probably feature her latest creations. Now, I need to obtain a much larger selection of her work so that I can map out a strategy for what to begin with and what to use in the follow-up show. These two shows will have to seem more like a retrospective than an exhibit reflecting her ongoing progress. We must be careful about this and make sure that both exhibits have her strongest work."

I stopped at this point and turned to Gary for a reaction. I thought surely he would like what I proposed. After all, I felt that I was presenting a plan that would give us the best shot at establishing his mother as an important contemporary artist.

"So what do you think of that strategy?" I asked optimistically.

Gary adjusted his necktie, which was clearly making him uncomfortable, and cleared his throat with a muffled cough. "So let me make sure I understand exactly what you're proposing. You want to wait for six months to mount an exhibit of my mother's work, and you don't want to show more than a small number of her paintings at that time. Then you want to wait another year before you put out more paintings for purchase. Is that correct?"

"Well, I guess you could put it that way," I replied hesitantly. "You see, what I'm trying to do is present Emma's work in such a way that I can gradually build her reputation. I frankly don't see another way of doing that. Surely, you agree that we want to do whatever we can to foster an understanding of her work, to create an environment that will encourage the art world to pay attention to what she has done."

I leaned forward again in order to make him understand the importance of what I had to say next. "Let me explain and make this clear. The art world is a very complex universe. I don't know if you noticed as you made your way here today, but within a ten block radius of where you sit right now there are more than three dozen galleries. Every one of those galleries has a group of artists that they are trying to market so they can sell their paintings for as much as possible. In the art world, to sell a painting means selling that artist's reputation. Every collector wants to think that they are buying a painting by the next Picasso."

Again I paused to gauge Gary's response. From the look on his face I had the feeling that he wasn't buying what I was saying, but I went on anyway, hoping to reach some sort of understanding.

"You may wonder," I began, "how do you go about building an artist's reputation? Well, I'm sorry to say that there is no easy answer to that question. But rest assured, every one of my colleagues is trying to figure that one out. We all know that it helps if you can get a little publicity. Maybe you can get the attention of an art critic, someone who writes for one of the more established newspapers or magazines that cover contemporary art. But you have to understand that these critics are literally bombarded with requests to review new shows. For every article that appears about a new and upcoming artist in - say - a publication like the New York Times, there are twenty, maybe thirty artists, who tried and failed to get the Times to write something about their show."

I then waved my arm in a gesture to indicate how enormous this whole process is. "And then," I continued, "even if you hit the jackpot and get some top critic to write about your artist, that article far from establishes their reputation. It's sad to say, but the public's memory is about as long as the time it takes them to drink a cup of coffee. As soon as the next bright sensation is introduced, there's fifteen more artists waiting in the wings. That's why you and I must remain diligent, we must reconcile ourselves to the fact that building a reputation is a long-term project, and the only way to do that is to carefully calculate each move and remain devoted to our goal."

Gary now shifted in his seat and looked out into the room. He seemed deep in thought, and there was a momentary silence in the conversation. "So," he finally replied, "if I'm understanding you correctly, there is no guarantee that you will ever be able to establish her reputation. You might mount a dozen exhibits of her work and still be left with an artist that is no better known than they are right now. Am I following you correctly?"

"Well yes," I replied, "that is true. But, as I said before, I think your mother's creative work is well worth the effort. She was an excellent painter, with an original vision. I was absolutely stunned the first time I saw her work, and I believe that other's will see what I saw."

He paused for a minute to think about what I said. "All of what you say is very interesting, but enough with all this high talk about artist's reputations, and how wonderful her vision was. I don't really care that much about it. Let's get down to what this is really all about. Obviously, if an artist has a good reputation their work sells for more. Is that not correct?"

I confirmed that it was.

"So what you want to do," he continued, "is to build her reputation so you can make more money off her work."

I could see where he was going, and it wasn't good. I decided to confront him head on. "Yes, I am running a business here, and I don't mind being able to sell a painting for more due to the fact that an artist has a good reputation. But let me point out, there are a lot of ways to make money easier than running an art gallery. I'm in this business because I love art, and I enjoy doing what I can to help deserving artists. Yes, I would profit more if your mother's paintings increased in value, but that's not my only priority. I like to think that we aren't just selling widgets here. We are selling something truly special, something that has social and cultural importance."

"Look," he began, "you can say all you want about the social and cultural importance of art, and how great my mother's paintings are. But let me be perfectly honest with you. I could care less about the art world, about reputations in the art world, and my mother's reputation, or lack of one. Knowing my mother all these years, I've been exposed to the art world more than most, and let me say in no uncertain terms, I have absolutely had my fill of artists and their world."

He shifted to the edge of his seat, and I could see that he was becoming somewhat agitated. "As far as I can see, artists are just a bunch of jerks with oversized egos. They all think that they're something special just because they throw paint on a canvas. I've seen how they do their thing. They can go on making speeches until everyone within hearing range is totally exhausted. They love using all kinds of obscure words, describing their unique vision in terms that no one else has the slightest idea what they're talking about. Of course, no one wants to look dumb, so they stand there, with a serious look on their face, nodding their heads up and down like they know exactly what this egomaniacal artist is spouting"

He shook his head in disgust. "They think the world owes them some special status because they paint, and they don't care about who they hurt in the process. It's clear you think my mother was so wonderful. I'm sure that when she visited you a couple of months ago the two of you had a grand time talking your art talk. She's very good at that. I've heard her talk about art more than once. She can play the role of creative genius with the best of them."

His voice grew more agitated with every word. "But let me come right out and say it - I hate her paintings. I know you think highly of them, and I'll bet the two of you could talk for an hour about some random brushstroke. And that's all fine for what it is, but come on, do you really think the rest of the world cares where she decides to fling paint. I'm sure that all of you in the art world are so very sophisticated, and can come up with all kinds of amazingly intelligent comments to make about the latest fashionable artist. But really, get off it! Do you really think that a bunch of brushstrokes slapped on a piece of canvas is really that earth-shattering."

He then let out a sarcastic smirk. "I don't want to be rude, but you people think that what you do is so important. I think you're all delusional. Every time she talked about art all I could think about was the story of the emperor with no clothes. Everyone wants to show how smart, how 'cultured' they are. But I wonder if it's all an act."

At this point I wanted to slap him and then walk away. But over the years I've learned to tolerate, and hold my tongue, when faced with people who seem to be unable, or unwilling, to understand art.

Now that he was on a roll he continued with abandon. "Let me tell you about another side of my mother that she doesn't talk about with other art people. Being into art, as I can see you are, will probably mean that what I'm about to tell you will seem utterly unsophisticated, but I'm going to tell you anyway. When I was just five years old, the person you think as so wonderful left my father - just walked out on him. She had been carrying on an affair with the lawyer she worked for at the time. Several afternoons a week they would leave work early and go fuck at his house. She was having a grand time until she messed up and got pregnant. My younger brother is almost certain that the man she was having the affair with is his real father. Who knows given the way she slept around."

He rolled his eyes in disgust. "After awhile, this man must have seen what she was really like and broke up with her. I must say I can't blame him. Then my mother, with no man to take care of her, went crying back to my father. I don't know what I would have done if I had faced his situation, but being the good man he was, he took her back and raised my brother as if he was his own son. He really took care of us over the years, especially during the times that my mother checked out of our lives to do her art thing.

"I can still remember when she returned from that trip to Chicago. I could tell that my father was just mystified by her, and was starting to get really frustrated with her constant comments about Abstract Expressionism. And you have to remember that my father was an educated man. He was a teacher. It wasn't like he didn't know anything about art. But my mother constantly acted like he was a total idiot. She never said it outright, but it was clear just from the way she looked at him.

"When she got the art bug it was like she had been struck by lightning on the road to Damascus. All we heard about for months was Abstract Expressionism this and Abstract Expressionism that. Let me tell you, I hated Abstract Expressionism before I had ever seen an Abstract Expressionist painting.

"And the paintings she began to make were awful. Please don't be offended, but as I walked into your gallery today, and I saw what you have on display, I could see that you're an enthusiast for a lot of weird art just like my mother's. So, my guess is that you would probably have liked her early paintings, but I thought they were terrible. My father called them her 'sling the paint' paintings."

At this point he flung himself back on the couch and laughed, shaking his head from side to side. Finally, he turned back to me with a big smile on his face. "I thought that description was perfect. My father had other colorful descriptions of her art. He described one painting as her 'oops, I spilled a can of paint on this one.' Another painting he described as 'her attempt to imitate the art of a toddler.' He went on to say that a toddler could have done better. I had a good laugh after that comment."

Then Gary's face changed and he took on a more serious demeanor. "Things got worse from there. She started doing paintings where you could just make out naked bodies, usually women. I couldn't believe that a woman would want to paint other naked women. These paintings were actually obscene, and she hung them around the house for every visitor, including children, to see. My father couldn't believe that she would actually show paintings like that, and tried to forbid her from displaying them, but there was no stopping her.

"When I was sixteen, and my younger brother was eleven, she just walked out on us and didn't even say goodbye. She just packed up in the middle of the night and left. When we woke up the next morning she was gone, just like that. Being an artist was more important to her than her own children. I didn't see her again for two years, and the only reason I saw her then was because I made the effort to go visit her.

"When I got there all she talked about was art. She said she made an effort to visit us. I don't believe it for a minute. I think she was just saying that to keep from seeming like the bad mother she was. I still wonder if her decision to leave was only about art."

"Let me stop you there," I interrupted. "I've been married twice, and I have a daughter. From my experience, I know that children don't always understand all that happens between a husband and a wife. Is it possible that maybe there were things that happened between your mother and father that you weren't aware of? Maybe some of your mother's actions stem from problems in the marriage."

I hoped to get him to think about his mother from a slightly different angle, but my effort was wasted. He just looked at me like I really didn't understand anything about his mother.

"I think she just wanted to sleep with other men," he stated bluntly" "I know for a fact that she was soon in bed with her art teacher. I'll bet she learned a lot about art while they fucked. To justify leaving, she went on and on about how she had no choice. I can still remember her lame line. 'Art chooses you, you don't choose it.' That's about the biggest bunch of bullshit I ever heard."

He then hesitated, and started talking about his college experience. I think he was trying to make me think he wasn't some hick from the country, although everything he said convinced me that that was exactly what he was.

"When I was in college I took an introduction to art history that covered European art from the Renaissance to the twentieth century, so its not like I don't know anything about art. I actually enjoyed the course. But we got a little behind and had to rush through the Modern art section. Our professor explained that, due to time constraints, he was forced to skip over some of the art movements of the twentieth century. I was glad. As far as I was concerned, the earlier periods, when artists were still creating art that wasn't so weird, was much more interesting to me. So, as far as I'm concerned, you can have your pretentious modern paint slingers. I'll stick with the masters of the past."

At this point he paused, took a deep breath, and gathered his thoughts. "So here's what I want you to do. This exhibit that you're so excited about, and that you want to put on in six months, is a perfect time to put all her art on display and sell it all. I want the money now, not three or four years from now. If you don't want to do that, as far as I'm concerned, your only other option is to buy all of her paintings now, and then you can do whatever you want with them. I could care less. I just want the money as quickly as I can get it. If there are suckers out there who are willing to buy her paintings then fine, I'll take their money. But don't waste my time talking about how we are going to build her reputation. I know who she really was."

After this rant I sat there in disbelief. I knew that there was nothing more to say. I wondered how this could happen. I know that art can be hard to understand, but why are family members so resentful of their artist relatives?

I quickly got down to business. "I need at least 60 of her paintings to be able to take the approach I want to take. I'll offer you $3,000 a painting. For 60 paintings that $90,000."

He responded immediately. "Make it an even $100,000 for 60 paintings and you have a deal."

"You have a deal," I replied without hesitation.

And with that he stood up and made his way out. I didn't even bother to walk him to the door. I asked my assistant to show him out. After he was gone I closed the door to my office and sat down at my desk. For the next hour I contemplated the price artists pay to make art. From the outside it must all seem so glamorous. The story of this artist should prove how wrong that image is.

A few weeks later I received the delivery of her paintings, and I sent Emma's son his check. Now the hard work of mounting an exhibit and trying to foster her reputation begins. Who knows how far I'll get. Will Emma Casland go down in history as one of the great artists of her time, or will she be forgotten along with the thousands of others who felt compelled to create art, but were condemned to obscurity?

Printed in the United States
By Bookmasters